W9-CAF-496

"Kelby Creek has an open wound."

Mel's voice was quiet. "I'm a walking, talking reminder that not all wounds are made by bad people. Sometimes they're made by people trying to pretend everything's okay."

Mel looked at Sterling and laid out her point.

"I never knew to stop Rider, but I do know how to stop being a constant reminder of him. Sterling, I never planned on coming back to Kelby Creek. Never."

When Sterling responded, his voice was hard.

"Then let's figure out why you're back and how the murder is connected. After that, you can go again and never look back."

It was what Mel wanted, yet she felt hesitation at the words.

Sterling's cool blue eyes bit into her.

She almost told him then—the real reason why she'd left town the way she had—but instead she nodded.

If Sterling knew Rider's last words to her before he'd gone to prison, he'd do something heroic.

And there was one thing Rider was very skilled at— destroying heroes.

So Mel kept her mouth shut.

ACCIDENTAL AMNESIA

—

TYLER ANNE SNELL

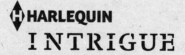

HARLEQUIN
INTRIGUE

If you purchased this book without a cover you should be aware that this book is stolen property. It was reported as "unsold and destroyed" to the publisher, and neither the author nor the publisher has received any payment for this "stripped book."

This book is for Kiddo. We met you for the first time while writing this book and we hope you're officially adopted by the time it releases. But, you know, don't actually read this book until you're older. Much older.

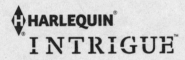

Recycling programs for this product may not exist in your area.

ISBN-13: 978-1-335-48959-3

Accidental Amnesia

Copyright © 2022 by Tyler Anne Snell

All rights reserved. No part of this book may be used or reproduced in any manner whatsoever without written permission except in the case of brief quotations embodied in critical articles and reviews.

This is a work of fiction. Names, characters, places and incidents are either the product of the author's imagination or are used fictitiously. Any resemblance to actual persons, living or dead, businesses, companies, events or locales is entirely coincidental.

For questions and comments about the quality of this book, please contact us at CustomerService@Harlequin.com.

Harlequin Enterprises ULC
22 Adelaide St. West, 41st Floor
Toronto, Ontario M5H 4E3, Canada
www.Harlequin.com

Printed in U.S.A.

R0462550023

Tyler Anne Snell genuinely loves all genres of the written word. However, she's realized that she loves books filled with sexual tension and mysteries a little more than the rest. Her stories have a good dose of both. Tyler lives in Alabama with her same-named husband and their mini "lions." When she isn't reading or writing, she's playing video games and working on her blog, *Almost There*. To follow her shenanigans, visit tylerannesnell.com.

Books by Tyler Anne Snell

Harlequin Intrigue

The Saving Kelby Creek Series

Uncovering Small Town Secrets
Searching for Evidence
Surviving the Truth
Accidental Amnesia

Winding Road Redemption

Reining in Trouble
Credible Alibi
Identical Threat
Last Stand Sheriff

The Protectors of Riker County

Small-Town Face-Off
The Deputy's Witness
Forgotten Pieces
Loving Baby
The Deputy's Baby
The Negotiation

Manhunt
Toxin Alert

Visit the Author Profile page at Harlequin.com.

CAST OF CHARACTERS

Sterling Costner—After returning home to Kelby Creek and the Dawn County Sheriff's Department, this deputy is ready for a new start. But when the woman who broke his heart all those years ago shows up with no memory and deadly danger around her every corner, he'll risk everything to protect her.

Melanie Blankenship—Waking with no memory within the town she swore she'd never return to again, this former public enemy of Kelby Creek must figure out why she came back and who wants her gone for good. But to survive the onslaught of danger that comes her way, she'll have to team up with her former lover to figure out the newest mystery in town.

Sam Costner—Little brother to Sterling and childhood best friend to Mel, he's quick to help no matter the danger involved.

Cole Reiner—This detective takes a critical eye to the events surrounding Mel's return, forcing Sterling and Mel deeper into the mystery.

Rider Partridge—Ex-husband to Mel, this charming businessman might be in prison, but his presence is still felt by all involved.

Jonathan Partridge—Brother to Rider, this shark of a lawyer isn't happy that Mel has returned home. And he makes sure she knows it.

Prologue

The members of the Dawn County Sheriff's Department in attendance were all wearing suits and dresses and had glasses of champagne, bottles of beer and small glasses filled with alcohol that burned when going down. Sheriff Chamblin was in the middle of the semicircle they'd made in the room and had his own whiskey neat lifted high.

"And this is to a lifetime of happiness with two of the best sleuths I know," he roared, cheeks red and a smile that covered his whole body staying strong. "Here's to our boy, Kenneth, and one of our favorite ladies, Willa!"

Everyone around them cheered, glasses clinking and laughter erupting when someone dropped their drink and someone else yelled, "Party foul."

It was an interesting sight, mostly because when Sterling Costner had left the department and his job, the people who had stayed felt the same as he had when he left town.

Betrayed. Angry. Broken.

Now here they were, celebrating the wedding of one of their detectives.

And doing so with a whole lot of noise and love.

He gave the sheriff an uncertain look when the older man's gaze swung to him as the crowd started to join the rest of the reception.

Brutus Chamblin, someone Sterling hadn't seen in a long while, was all gray now. Though Brutus had mostly been gray before he'd come out of retirement, maybe now there was a weight there that Sterling hadn't seen previously and it was throwing him off.

Brutus looked tired. Tired all the way down to his bones.

Even through the smile he greeted Sterling with.

"Sterling Costner, as I live and breathe."

They clasped hands before Sterling pulled the man in for a hug. He'd always been a fan of Brutus's.

"I didn't know you were back in town," Brutus said, pulling his cowboy hat off and pressing it against his chest. Out of all the employees of the sheriff's department that Sterling had known before he'd left town, only Brutus had liked wearing a cowboy hat.

Other than Sterling, of course.

He pulled his own down, too, and thumped it against his thigh as they talked.

"I came in last week to get settled and hang out with my brother," Sterling started. "I was hoping to catch up with you next week, but then Carlos caught wind of me. He dragged me here as his plus-one. Though, between you and me, I'm pretty sure I stopped existing the moment he saw Dr. Alvarez in that frilly dress." They both grinned at that. Carlos Park was a longtime sheriff's department deputy, which was a rare thing given what had happened five years prior. Not many people had stuck around. Sterling was ashamed to say he was one of those who had hightailed it away.

Though his reasons had been a little more personal.

"I have to say I'm glad he wanted to bring me along," Sterling added. "I wouldn't have believed the warm fuzzies coming from the department that I just witnessed had I not seen it with my own eyes."

At that, Brutus seemed to become younger in spirit. He was beaming.

"I hate to say anything against the men and women from when I was sheriff the first time around, but I don't think I've ever been prouder of a group of people than I am with this lot. They've done some amazing things for the department and the town against some stacked odds."

Sterling nodded. The shame of leaving buried deeper, but he refocused on why he was here.

Brutus stayed quiet, most likely knowing he was at the waiting end of the conversation. For a moment they watched as the last wedding guests left the room.

Then it was just the two of them and their future.

"I'm back, Brutus," Sterling said. "For good."

Brutus looked him up and down and then nodded.

He put on his cowboy hat, a worn brown leather Stetson.

"Things have changed around here," he warned. "Not all for the good, sad to say. We might have won back some trust from the town, but there's still a lot of unsettled things. It won't be easy. The fix won't be quick, either. Might be years before any real progress is made."

"No way to know until we do it."

Sterling put emphasis on the *we* part.

That seemed to be enough.

"Come in tomorrow for an official interview," Brutus said. "After that I'll introduce you to the people who have moved in since you left. Maybe even take you out for a drink later so you can see some of the things in town that look a whole lot different, too."

Sterling couldn't help but grin.

"I can swing that."

"Good."

Brutus gave him another widening smile and clapped him on the back.

"Welcome back to Kelby Creek, Sterling Costner."

Sterling put his cowboy hat back on.

"It's good to be back."

He said the words, but Sterling hoped he wasn't lying.

Chapter One

Three months later and Deputy Sterling Costner had fire in his eyes and anger on his tongue.

Anyone in Kelby Creek, Alabama, could see it if they were so inclined. Sterling was an open book in a cowboy hat. An open book in a cowboy hat with a flashlight on it and narration available. He didn't keep things close to the vest, unlike some of his Dawn County Sheriff's Department colleagues.

Nope. He was what his brother, Sam, called an expresser. A bullhorn with the button stuck to *on*. He didn't brood—he projected.

He was also a man who wasn't about to let someone who called themselves Top Tier give him any more lip than he'd already given him during the house call.

"Listen, I'm not standing here on your doorstep, wearing this uniform despite the heat, humidity and the fact that I had to skip lunch to be here, because I'm a glutton for punishment," Sterling said, looking down his nose at the young man. "I came because two neighbors complained that your music was so loud it was making their windows vibrate. That needs to stop."

For some people, Top Tier might have been a nickname that painted a picture of a towering, muscled person, but the twenty-two-year-old standing in front of Sterling fell woefully short of that image. He was small, thin and had a little squeak to his voice despite his immediate and continued defiance against Sterling from the get-go.

Though his size and name wouldn't have mattered at all had he not spoken ill of Sterling's partner. Once he'd called Marigold a nosy you-know-what, all civility had frolicked off into the South Alabama heat. Which was why Sterling wasn't in the mood to listen to any more of the man's ranting.

So he underlined his point.

"You need to turn the music down or else there are going to be some real consequences for you, no matter what name you give me." Another reason Sterling had been called a bullhorn was due to how deep his voice was. Never mind when he was trying to make sure he got a point across. Top Tier seemed to consider it more than he had when they'd first met. "But that's only if you apologize to my partner for being indecent. Do you understand or do we need to escalate this situation?"

Top Tier wavered, but only for a moment.

He took a small step to the side and nodded to Marigold, who was farther back on the sidewalk, looking two kinds of angry and one kind of bored.

"I'm—I'm sorry," Top Tier called out. "I think I drank too many 5-hour Energy drinks today."

Sterling wasn't about to ask what that had to do with being decent, but he let it slide. They were only there for a noise complaint, after all.

"I accept," Marigold responded.

Sterling looked back to Top Tier.

"All right, now what happens next for you?"

Top Tier thumbed back to the house behind him.

"I turn my video game down to an acceptable volume," he answered, repeating Marigold's original request before the young man had started calling her names. "Right?"

"Right," Sterling confirmed. "And no time like the present."

Sterling waited as Top Tier hustled inside. Marigold joined him on the porch.

"His real name is Anthony, you know?" she muttered. "My sister babysat him a few times when she was in high school. He was a twerp then, and he's a twerp now. 'Top Tier.'" She snorted. Sterling kept a straight face until the music had gone silent. When that held, they went back to their SUV.

"Hey, reinvention isn't always a clean process," he said. "Some people just miss the mark. We shouldn't judge the attempt."

Marigold crossed her arms but laughed.

"I mean he did call me the B-word, so I'm going to judge a little."

He joined in and pulled out onto the street.

"Fair enough."

Apart from the noise complaint, Kelby Creek, Alabama, was mostly quiet on that Monday. The weather was playing nice, too, or at least nicer than it had been the week before. Hot and humid but with a breeze. Best you could ask for, considering.

Sterling pointed his cruiser in the direction of the north side of Kelby Creek.

Marigold seemed to pick up on his thoughts.

"We're grabbing lunch from that new food truck? The one with the tacos that Rossi hasn't stopped talking about?"

"Unless you want to hit the lunch crowd at Crisp's."

Marigold mock shuddered. Her former mother-in-law owned every local's favorite restaurant in town. While Marigold had been justified in ending her marriage, her ex's mother had never been quiet about her displeasure that it happened.

And that displeasure from a Southern woman translated into passive-aggressive comments and actions.

Which made everyone around uncomfortable.

"Tacos, it is."

They fell into a conversation about Top Tier, another about a cold case that the task force was working at the moment and then about when they thought Kelby Creek would see its first tornado of the year.

It was only when he realized he'd taken the long way round to the food truck stop that Sterling fell quiet.

Marigold noticed. She was good with body language and sensing shifting moods. It was one of the reasons she'd been hired the year before and why Sterling had been glad to be partnered with her. She was good at her job, but she was also good at people.

She nodded out the window.

They were passing a small neighborhood situated around two streets that ended in cul-de-sacs.

"Did you mean to take us this way or was it a subconscious thing?"

Sterling, the human bullhorn, didn't lie.

"I wasn't thinking about it, so I'm guessing it was a subconscious thing." He sighed and kept his eyes firmly on the street ahead. Marigold tried to be sympathetic.

"Hey, sometimes it doesn't matter how much time has passed. Some things just stick."

She meant "some people," and by that she meant "a particular woman," but Marigold kept it vague for his sake.

Normally, he would have admitted that they were both talking about someone who had once lived in that neighborhood, but nothing in Kelby Creek was that normal anymore.

Instead Sterling turned down the volume on his bullhorn thoughts and switched gears to what he was thinking about ordering for lunch. Marigold threw in her two cents, and soon that neighborhood was in his rearview. Along with the house Sterling had once lived in.

And the woman who had lived there with him.

Before she'd destroyed everything.

Before she'd destroyed him.

Sterling didn't even glance back once as they drove away.

Because, as much as he'd tried to forget her, Melanie Blankenship never stayed in his rearview for long.

MEL KNEW SHE was in trouble. There were just no two ways about it.

She opened her eyes and tried to answer several questions all at once.

Why was she lying down?

Why was she wet?

Why was it so hot?

What was that noise?

Where was she?

She groaned, unable to answer any of them.

Movement entered the list of things sending her into sensory overload.

Mel finally opened her eyes to find a woman hovering over her, concern clear in her drawn brow.

"Hey, can you hear me? My name is Anna." Mel tried to sit up, as if the new position could help her process the information faster. Instead all it did was make her wince as pain shot up her side. The woman named Anna gently pushed her back down. "Take it easy. You were in an accident. We're in an ambulance on the way to the hospital to make sure you're okay. Do you understand?"

Mel didn't.

Her head hurt as much as it was confused.

Though that confusion started lifting when she heard someone over a radio chirp out the name of said hospital.

Mel struggled to sit up again.

"Wait. Where am I?" Mel asked.

The gentle pressure of Anna's hands managed to push her back down.

"In the back of an ambulance, on the way to the—"

"No, *where* are we? What town?" Mel interrupted.

Anna's look of concern seemed to double down on itself.

Mel didn't care.

She *did* care about what was said next.

Anna had the audacity to make the answer sound casual.

"We're heading into Kelby Creek."

This time Mel didn't need help staying down.

Instead she closed her eyes tight and swore.

"You should have left me where you found me."

THE NEXT TIME Melanie Blankenship opened her eyes, the world had once again seemingly changed all at once.

This time, at least, she could remember the point B that had led to this point C. But how she'd gotten from point A to that point B?

Foggy.

Blank.

She'd been in the ambulance.

She was at the hospital now.

Everything else?

Might as well have been cotton candy beneath running water.

"I have amnesia?"

Mel's doctor, a graying man who must have been a hoot for children based on how many times he'd used the word *noggin* and how often he chuckled at the sight of blood, laughed lightly.

"Temporary memory loss due to a traumatic event," he said, not for the first time. He pointed to the bandage on Mel's hairline. "Thanks to the impact of being in a car accident."

Mel went to touch the bandage again, but the doctor was quick. He gently took her hand and steered it away from the wound.

"Like you said, it appears to be short-term loss only, and, as frustrating as that can be, let's count our blessings that it isn't worse." The childish grin he'd been wearing since he'd come in to see her became more serious. "Rest, give it time and the memories should come back. Your body just needs time to heal."

"Should? Not will?"

The doctor had the good sense to look apologetic.

"Everyone's different. There's a chance you might not get every detail back but, hey, thankfully you only seem to have lost less than a day. Luckily, not too much time in the grand scheme of things."

Considering Mel had woken up in an ambulance in Kelby Creek, she very much disagreed. Her fewer than twenty-four hours had packed a punch.

She just didn't know where that punch had come from or why she'd been punched at all.

Mel had about 2.3 billion questions left to ask, but the headache that the meds hadn't dismantled kept all of them behind her lips.

"Now, I'll ask again," started the doctor. "Are you sure there isn't anyone you want us to call? The nurse said you were insistent against your current emergency contact, but now that you've had time to settle?"

Mel shook her head too quickly. She winced, then tried to play through the show of pain.

"I'm good, thanks."

The doctor hesitated a moment but then let it lie. He was back to a big smile. Then he was gone.

Mel took the moment after to try to dig deep again.

What had happened in the last day?

Sunday she had been at her apartment in Birmingham, finishing an article when...

She was packing a bag and getting into her car...

Then it was Monday afternoon and she was in a hospital hours away.

Mel groaned.

It was like trying to recall a dream. The attempt itself was making the memory harder to grasp.

She kicked her legs over the edge of the hospital bed and hit the ground running, so to speak. Mel shimmied back into her jeans beneath the hospital gown. Her bra and blouse weren't going to go through the same motions. Since the ambulance had picked her up and the paramedics had been unable to wake her right away, they'd cut her shirt and bra wide-open. Now both were in the garbage bin.

At the very least, the first responders had grabbed her purse.

Mel, not for the first time, went to it and through it quickly.

Nothing seemed out of place. At least not what she'd considered normal before her memory had decided to fragment.

Her cell phone was even resting inside—no missed or outgoing calls during her memory lapse. No texts, either.

For some people the lack of communication from friends or family would have been concerning. For Mel it was oddly comforting.

Whatever had happened between Sunday and that Monday had at least not concerned anyone else.

Well, that she remembered.

Mel straightened and slowly looked around the hospital room.

There had to be a reason she'd pointed her car toward Kelby Creek.

The one place she'd sworn to never visit again.

"Why now?"

The hospital room didn't answer her, and she decided staying wouldn't get her any answers, either. Mel had spent too much of her life being in the dark. Being oblivious. That wasn't her anymore.

She needed to figure out what was going on.

Resolved to calling a coworker from their home decor magazine *P's & Q's* to see if anything had happened there, Mel readied to leave.

A knock on the door, however, stopped her in her tracks.

Her heartbeat sped up.

There were many reasons why Mel didn't want to be back in Kelby Creek.

When the door opened to show a man staring at her, she felt a pit of nerves bunch in her stomach.

He definitely was one of the reasons why she'd never wanted to cross the town limits again.

"Jonathan."

Jonathan Partridge was exactly three things: a true platinum blond, a lover of freshly pressed suits and a terrifying lawyer. The fact that he was only a few years younger than Mel somehow made him more menacing than if he'd been more seasoned.

It didn't help that he was her former brother-in-law

and, unless something had changed since she'd been gone, not at all a fan of hers.

"What are you doing here?" she asked before he could start in.

Mel smoothed down her hospital gown as Jonathan smiled.

Shark's teeth.

And he looked like he'd already smelled blood in the water.

"Small town, fast news." He shrugged and sauntered over. If someone wasn't sure of the man's worth, he made sure to act like he was top-shelf quality at all times. Everyone else? Expired off-brand. "It didn't take long to hear about a nasty wreck out at the town limits and a woman being taken to the hospital. It certainly didn't take long for the name of that woman to travel faster than the rest of the details."

He stopped at the foot of the hospital bed. Even though Mel was standing on the opposite side of it, she felt vulnerable with him there.

She didn't like it.

Jonathan shook his head a little. He chuckled.

"Mel Blankenship. I have to say, I'm surprised on many fronts," he continued. "You being back in town was enough, but then to hear you'd been at the receiving end of a nasty hit-and-run with nothing more than a packed suitcase in the trunk? And now, to top it all off, you're allegedly having memory problems? Wow. Color me— Well, color me surprised. I guess there isn't another word for it."

Mel felt the heat in her face. She knew she was turning a nasty shade of red.

Just as she knew that letting her rising anger out at Jonathan was a dangerous game that she didn't want to play.

It was true, he wasn't as cunning as his brother, but underestimating how crafty the youngest Partridge was would be a mistake she wasn't going to add to her life's list of regrets.

"Surprised or not, me being back is none of your business." She kept her voice even. It was a difficult move.

Jonathan shrugged again.

This time he put his hands into the motion, turning his palms up to the ceiling. Whether or not he did so to showcase the burn scars on his skin, she didn't know.

"It might not be my business, but it is my concern." His cheeky smile deepened into a frown. He dropped his hands at this side. "The last time you were in Kelby Creek, you almost cost me everything. I don't want a repeat performance."

Mel didn't know why she'd come back to Kelby Creek, but in that moment she wished she could remind herself how bad an idea it had been.

There was "disliked by the general public" and then there was "hated by enough individuals that crossing the town limits wasn't just dumb, it was a gamble."

Why had she made it?

What had she hoped to gain?

"I don't want any trouble," she decided on when it was clear that Jonathan was remaining rooted to the spot. "After I get my things and a ride, I'm leaving."

Jonathan gave her a long, cool stare.

It made her skin crawl.

Yet, for all the things she didn't like about Jonathan, one thing she was grateful for about him was that he looked nothing like his brother.

Small blessings and all that.

"And what about the house?"

She felt her body stiffen in defense.

Mel didn't want to talk with him or anyone about the house.

Jonathan's gaze scanned her up and down quickly.

In turn he tensed.

Mel wanted to avoid a fight, but she wasn't about to be corralled into a trap.

"We're no longer family, and we were certainly never friends," she started. "There's no reason for you to be here, especially now that you've said your bitter little piece. And that's exactly what I'll say to the authorities if you don't leave now." Mel took a small step forward and crossed her arms over her chest. "And before you remind me of why that would be a bad idea, since the sheriff's department and the town aren't crazy about me, let me remind *you*. I may be Rider Partridge's ex-wife, but you're his brother, and around these parts blood is thicker than water."

Mel imagined she was a tree that had been growing roots all the years she'd been gone. Roots that were worn and weathered but tough.

Stronger than any Partridge man's.

She didn't move an inch while Jonathan went through his emotions in silence.

There was anger. There was regret. There was more anger.

Then there was blazing blame written clearly across his scowl.

But she wasn't wrong.

"Kelby Creek isn't the same as it was when you left," he said, already angling toward the door. "There are a lot scarier things lurking in the shadows now. I suggest you don't go looking for any of them."

Mel watched as Jonathan and his fancy suit slithered back out in the hallway.

Instead of taking the moment after to breathe, she doubled down on her plan of leaving the hospital.

And then Kelby Creek. This time for good.

Chapter Two

The sunset was probably nice, but Sterling wasn't pay-ing it any attention. He'd seen Southern sunsets before, knew they had a look to them that made you want to paint them. Just as he knew that today's sunset was probably particularly nice. No clouds in the sky and a nice breeze across the ground. In fact, he wouldn't be surprised at all if his brother, Sam, didn't send him a picture of it from his back porch with a caption of a smiley-face emoji with hearts around it.

But Sterling wasn't looking at the sky when he got out of his truck.

He wasn't looking at the oranges and purples and pinks hanging above him as he patted down his shirt or straightened his cowboy hat.

He surely wasn't trying to see the stars peeking out, ready to shine for the night.

Instead, his focus and thoughts had all but narrowed on a woman.

Sterling had practiced during the ride over to the hos-pital what he'd say and do when he first saw Melanie after all these years—something he'd actually practiced before throughout those same years—but he couldn't seem to find anything that felt right.

That made what she'd done, how he'd felt about it and the last five years feel better.

"You sure you should be going there at all?" Marigold had asked when the call had come through from the sheriff. "Like the sheriff said, it can be one of us that goes. You don't owe her anything."

"Melanie isn't just my ex," he'd responded, trying to be delicate. "Her history with this town is complicated. Better me go than someone who hasn't had the time to deal with their feelings about her. It's simpler if I go."

Marigold hadn't been satisfied with the answer.

"I'd say what happened between you two is nothing but complicated."

Sterling didn't dispute that, but he had left, focus narrowing.

All he had to do was ask Melanie a few questions and give her the suitcase she'd left in the trunk of her car.

Then he could leave and go back to not seeing her again.

Nothing complicated with that.

A simple plan.

One as easy as not looking up at the sunset.

And one that didn't last past the sidewalk.

"Oh, excuse me."

A woman wearing a hospital gown hurried out of the hospital's front doors and ran smack-dab into Sterling's shoulder. It took him half a second to realize she had the gown tucked into jeans like it was a shirt. It took him the other half of that second to realize that gown was a cool ways south from a pair of truer than true ice-blue eyes.

Ones that made you forget about the world.

"Mel?"

The woman's eyes widened, but he didn't need any confirmation from her.

Sometimes a minute felt like a lifetime, and then sometimes five years felt like no time had passed at all.

Melanie Blankenship looked like she did the day she'd left.

Beautiful from head to toe.

Coal-black hair always wrapped up into something messy, a button nose that scrunched when she was being mischievous or when she thought something was particularly great, and a dimple in her chin that made her acts of defiance that much more defiant. The freckles that had been a complement to her tanned-skin growing up were maybe a bit more pronounced, but she probably hadn't been sunbathing like she used to since she'd left Kelby Creek.

Then again, time *had* passed between them. Even when it felt like it hadn't.

Sterling was reminded of that fact when Mel took a quick step back from him, mouth dropping open.

"Sterling."

Two syllables jam-packed with the sound of regret.

And it wasn't regret at their past but at seeing him now.

That much he could pick up on quicker than a sunset could be beautiful.

"I— Sorry," she hurriedly tacked on. "I just didn't

expect to see you. Here. I told the nurse I didn't want them to call anyone."

Sterling tilted his head a little.

"The nurses didn't call me. I'm here for the department." He tapped his badge. "You were in a pretty serious accident where the other party left the scene. I'm here to take a statement."

Mel's face darkened a shade.

"Oh. Yeah, okay."

She touched the bunched-up fabric of her gown.

Sterling looked around at the parking lot behind them.

"Is someone here to pick you up?"

Mel shook her head. It was hard not to look at the bandage on it. When the news had come in about the accident and the victim having issues with her memory, it had been interesting enough. When the sheriff heard that it was Mel, everything had changed.

Sterling felt the familiar pull of anger toward someone who had dared to hurt the woman in front of him.

He tried to keep things professional.

"Then why are you running away?"

So much for professional. At his own question, he felt another familiar pull. This time toward his own anger. His own confusion and resentment.

One minute into seeing Mel and he was back to waiting on that front porch for a woman who wasn't coming.

"From the hospital," Sterling added. "I heard about your head, and I can't imagine they'd just let you leave."

At that, Mel snorted.

It was unlike her.

"All they're giving me in there is ibuprofen and making sure I don't have any reactions to anything. I can do that where I don't have to worry about unwanted visitors."

"Unwanted visitors? Someone already giving you trouble?"

There again was that anger toward someone else for her sake.

Sometimes those five years really did feel like nothing.

Mel shook out her shoulders a little. She cast her gaze out to the parking lot as she answered.

"Jonathan just came by and was his usual charming self."

Sterling grumbled on reflex. He'd never been a fan of Jonathan Partridge.

"Did he threaten you?"

At that Mel met his eye. She looked more annoyed than scared. Still, he thought he heard some hesitance.

"He was being Jonathan and talking out of his suit. I told him to beat it or I'd call in the department myself, and he scurried out fast. You know me—I don't suffer Jonathan Partridge long if I can help it."

Sterling had thought he'd known everything there was to know about Melanie Blankenship at one point in their lives. From her favorites to her dislikes to the subtle things she did that she did subconsciously.

He thought he'd known her, full body and soul.

Then she'd gone, a simple text in her wake that read, I'm sorry, Sterling. I hope you have a good life.

How had he not seen that coming?

And did that mean he hadn't known her at all?

Keep it simple, he told himself with force. *This doesn't have to be anything complicated.*

Sterling cleared his throat.

"Well, if you're on your way out, then why don't you come by the department tomorrow for your statement? That is, assuming you're staying in town." He pointed back to his truck. "I have your packed suitcase they found in the trunk of your car, so I was guessing you might be."

At this Mel's entire demeanor changed. Though for the life of him he couldn't figure out what emotion was making that change.

"I'm staying the night," she said. "Just need to call a cab and get a ride since, apparently, my car has seen much better days."

Sterling shouldn't have said it.

But he did.

"I can give you a ride. I know the town, and it'll be a lot faster than waiting for Grant to drive over here."

Mel's eyebrow rose. She didn't turn him down, though.

"That would actually be a big help. Thanks."

FIVE YEARS OF memories didn't compare an ounce to the man they'd been made about. Not when he seemingly materialized out of midair wrapped in a uniform that fit nicely, topped with a cowboy hat his daddy had given him and carrying some emotions behind clear blue eyes.

Eyes that, once they found Mel during her attempt to flee the hospital, never strayed.

Not that she'd expected anything but full attention when Sterling Costner found out she was back in town.

Though, silly ol' Mel had been hoping that she'd have more time before she had *this* face-to-face.

Because, as much as she was hoping no one else would catch wind of her arrival, she knew the gossip mill around town was probably already aflame. Not just Jonathan and his sketchy connections.

"I'm glad this wasn't destroyed," Mel said lamely once she slid into the passenger seat, picking up her suitcase in the process. She placed it on her lap.

She remembered leaving her apartment with it but not what she'd packed inside. At least now she could change out of her hospital gown.

Sterling slid into his truck like a knife through butter.

The man could make anything look good.

"I didn't see your car, but Deputy Rossi said it looked like someone hit your back end," he said once the door was shut. "Then you most likely spun out and hit the ditch, causing you to flip. Whoever hit you probably got spooked and took off. We're looking for them, though, so don't worry."

Mel's stomach moved a little at that last part.

"Don't worry" in Sterling's voice used to be the soundtrack to her life. A comforting repetition that felt like it could fix everything.

But there was no time for that now.

She played with the zipper on her suitcase.

"I guess I'll deal with the technical stuff tomorrow. Not sure what my insurance is going to say about the whole situation. I suppose it depends on how many cases of *amnesia* they get."

Sterling shrugged. He was such a big man that even the most subtle movements drew attention.

"I'm sure you'll do fine with them," he said. "You've always been a grade-A talker."

Mel snorted at that.

"Out of everyone in my life, I've been the least charming of them all. It took me almost a year to convince my neighbor to call me Mel. If I can't get someone to call me by my preferred name, then I don't think I can be counted as a grade-A anything."

Like his shrug, Mel noticed Sterling straighten.

She decided talking about her past was as bad as talking about theirs, so she looked out the window and tried to pretend for a moment that nothing had changed.

That she hadn't married Rider Partridge.

That she hadn't waited so long to divorce him.

That she hadn't fallen in love with Sterling.

That she hadn't—

Mel sat up straighter.

She glanced at Sterling and found him already looking at her.

She smiled.

It wasn't returned.

They both went to looking back out of the windshield.

"Where are we headed?" he asked.

Another simple thing that felt unbelievably weighted. The answer would feel that much more uncomfortable because, while going to a motel made sense, the moment

Jonathan had asked her about her old home had been the moment Mel had decided it was time to go back.

Even if it was the last place she wanted to go.

THE HOUSE COULD have been a home. If only Rider Partridge hadn't made it to out be a castle for his throne instead.

In retrospect, Mel saw it for what it was. She understood now that Rider hadn't wanted a family, a place to belong, like her back then. He'd wanted a kingdom for the townspeople to wish was theirs. He wanted power in every way. Visible like his castle, but subtle, too. So subtle that no one realized it until it was too late.

Mel looked at the two-story almost-mansion and took a small amount of pleasure at seeing the weeds that had popped up along the sprawling lawn, the gutters that needed cleaning and the various spots of mold across the custom shutters. There were a few missing shingles, too, no doubt from a rough storm, and one of the windows from the second floor had lost its screen.

Not a derelict building, but certainly not the pearl in the oyster Rider had paid so much to build.

That small satisfaction at something he'd loved so much wilting just a smidge lasted as long as a breath.

But, for Mel, it was a good breath.

"You can call down to the auto shop tomorrow to see if Frank can give you a better idea of your car situation." Sterling appeared at her side, eyes on her and not the house. "Not too sure how that will shake out. Frank isn't as fast as he used to be when you were here last. Since his hip replacement, he's let his nephew do more and more, but, well, you know Frank. He's a helicopter boss. He'll tell you to go at something and then come back and just do it himself in the end."

Mel nodded, because she did know how Frank was. He'd been that way since they were teens, riding around with their busted cars and not a care in the world.

Now it was different. They were different, so the nod was enough.

Sterling pulled her suitcase up and started to walk it to the front door. The last time they'd done the same song and dance, it had been in the opposite direction.

Five years ago.

A lifetime ago.

Sterling stopped at the top step of the porch. Mel passed by him, key out.

"There's an alarm that I have to go in and type a code into," she warned. "If not, all the bells and whistles will start going off and the department will be called. I... would like to avoid that."

Sterling nodded this time. He was tracing the porch with his eyes. Mel couldn't read anything on him other than mild disinterest.

Which meant his poker face must have gotten a whole lot better in the last few years, or else he was really over what had happened.

Rider. The house. Her.

Which would be a good thing, Mel reminded herself. *No reason for him to still be on about you. Just like you're not on about him. Get it together. Bigger fish.*

The door unlocked with ease. As soon as it swung open, a beeping started. Mel hustled in and hurried straight through the grand foyer to the kitchen at the back of the house. The keypad lit up under her fingers as she typed in the code.

The beeping stopped when she hit Enter, but she took a moment to hover.

It had been a long time since she'd been in this kitchen. Like the rest of the house, it was grand and upscale. Brand-new, barely used appliances, top-notch countertops and fixtures, and a pantry that was half the size of her apartment in Birmingham now. It also was the one room in the house that had more doors than the rest.

One led outside to the covered brick patio, one led into the office, the one she'd come through went back to the foyer and then the last one, tucked next to the pantry, led downstairs to the basement.

Mel's gaze stuck to that door now.

She knew nothing that had or would ever happen was because of that door, yet every time she saw it she felt nothing but anger, resentment and guilt.

If it would have done any good, she would have punched it. Taken an ax to it. Thrown it into the wood chipper and had a glass of wine as she watched it disintegrate.

But she wouldn't do any of that.

It was just a door, after all.

It hadn't kidnapped a young girl, taken her to the basement below and held her there for two days.

It hadn't been oblivious upstairs, unaware that her husband was an actual monster, letting it happen, either.

So Mel let that anger, that hurt and shame, simmer

and went back through to the foyer and to the only man who had never blamed her for what had happened in that basement.

Sterling whistled low and motioned to the staircase. It curved up and around to the second-floor landing.

"I forgot how fancy this place is," he said. "It looks like it belongs in a magazine."

Mel snorted.

"It belongs somewhere, but definitely not a magazine."

The way she said it must have keyed him into some of what she was feeling. He set her suitcase down. By the scrunch of his brow, she knew what was coming next.

"Why don't you sell it? Surely the upkeep isn't worth it at the very least."

Mel sighed.

"I have enough from the settlement that the upkeep doesn't bother me a bit."

Sterling took a small step forward and motioned around them.

"But the house does."

It wasn't a question. So she didn't give him an answer. Instead Mel smiled and ignored.

Two things she'd proven to be too good at in the past.

"Thank you for the ride, Sterling. I mean it. I'll come to the department tomorrow to give my statement."

She didn't move an inch. Sterling's eyes—had they been that blue before?—settled on hers.

He opened his mouth but didn't say anything right away.

For a moment they were just two people standing in

a room with a slight echo, the only thing between them a past too complicated to talk about. At least, for her.

"Okay," he finally said. Sterling gave the room one last look around. Then a small nod before meeting her eye again. "I hope this all works out for you. Whatever it is you're doing, Mel."

Mel went with polite but to the point, the only response she could at the moment.

"Thank you. I shouldn't be here long."

Then the cowboy deputy left without another look or word.

Mel's stomach dropped a little, but she shut the door behind him and threw the dead bolt.

She might not remember why she was back in town, but she knew enough to avoid bringing Sterling into her problems again.

Chapter Three

Marigold was abuzz when Sterling got back to the sheriff's department.

"You gotta give me a minute before I talk," he was quick to say. "I'm boiling beneath my collar, and I need to cool down before I say something I'll regret."

They were in the break room, both already having ended their shifts. Marigold had coffee in her hand. The other coffee had been handed to Sterling upon his arrival. It wasn't something they often did—drink the stuff—but he couldn't deny it might help with the headache clustering behind his eyes.

Sterling would always give it to Marigold—she was good at reading people.

He drank a few long pulls and then put his cowboy hat down on one of the tabletops. His father, Callahan, had gifted it to him on his eighteenth birthday. It gave him some comfort. Enough so that he was ready to talk.

He still couldn't believe that no more than twenty minutes ago he'd been staring at Mel. A ghost from his past come back to haunt him. A ghost who had grabbed all of his attention, only to tell him she wouldn't be wailing through town for long. Not that he could believe her on that one, either. Mel couldn't remember why she was in town so how would she know how long she was staying?

Sterling clenched his jaw, frustrated for every reason in the book.

Then he let out a long, loud breath.

Marigold watched, quiet, but he could see some questions behind her eyes.

"All right," he decided. "Ask whatever it is you want to know, because I know you're not here just to give my sorry self some caffeine."

Marigold straightened but didn't defend herself.

"I'd be offended at the implication that I hung around just to get information out of you. If it wasn't true… Now, I know the bare bones of your past with Ms. Blankenship and her connection to what happened in town, *but* I think I'm missing some more nuanced details. At least based on how Deputy Juliet acted when she heard that Melanie was back in town. And I'll be honest, she wasn't the first person around here who I saw tense at the gossip."

Sterling dropped his head a little and swore.

He hadn't thought about how others close to him might react to Mel's sudden reappearance.

"Juliet's brother left town after what happened to try and get a more respectable job," Sterling explained. "He was killed in a car accident shortly after. He was all Juliet had in the way of family."

"But how exactly is that Melanie Blankenship's fault?"

It was a simple question, but there was never a simple answer when it came to what had happened almost six years ago to Kelby Creek during what the locals still referred to as The Flood.

"It's easier to blame Mel for what Rider Partridge did, since he's in prison." Sterling looked around and lowered his voice, not wanting to trigger anyone else. "Tell me everything you know about the story of Annie McHale and I'll tell you something you don't know."

Marigold raised her eyebrow but was game.

"Beloved daughter of the even more beloved McHale family goes missing six years ago and the entire town pulls together to find her," she recited. "A few days later, kidnappers send a hefty ransom demand, and the sheriff convinces the McHales to use it as a way to ambush them and get Annie back. But instead several people were killed and injured in a shoot-out where the kidnappers got away. Then the case caught national attention when the kidnappers hacked the town's website and posted a video of Annie tied up and bloody, where they demanded more money or else. That's also when the FBI became serious about it."

He nodded as she continued.

"Two agents came to town to investigate. One agent said she found a lead before that agent disappeared. When her partner went looking for her, he got caught during a flash flood, where he happened upon the mayor, who had crashed into a ditch. While the agent tried to help him, he stumbled upon Annie McHale's necklace in the back seat. The agent decided to dig deeper into the mayor after that and found out he *and* the sheriff were behind Annie's kidnapping. But that's not where the corruption stopped. Or started."

People said misery loved company, but corruption was the real people person. After a new FBI task force had come specifically for the town, Kelby Creek had been forever changed. Cases of corruption surfaced that had come way before Annie's kidnapping and spread a lot further than anyone had imagined. It turned the town against local law enforcement and government officials. Anyone with authority, really. The guilty were arrested, killed in attempted apprehension or, for a few, fled. Those who weren't guilty transferred, quit or stayed with new chips on their shoulders.

It was why Brutus was the sheriff now and why he'd spent every day since his appointment trying to find good men and women to redeem the tarnished name of the department.

It was also why Marigold had, in part, applied to become a deputy after a few years in the business world. She'd told Sterling she wanted to do something good but only do it around other people trying to do the same thing.

Sterling wasn't about to tell her he wasn't exactly sure if he qualified as one of those people. He had left after the investigations had ended and the department was crippled and in the most need, after all.

"So everyone knows the main players of The Flood," he said. "The sheriff, the mayor, hell, even the coroner got the spotlight for a good while. But you know the saying 'behind every successful man, there's a strong woman'? Well, behind every corrupt man, there's an even more corrupt one holding it together."

Marigold picked up on what he was saying.

"Rider Partridge, Mel's ex-husband," she guessed.

Sterling nodded.

"The sheriff and mayor were all flashy and shiny so everyone looked at them at first, but then the FBI started to realize that they would have needed serious help with Annie, not to mention their less-than-legal adventures before her kidnapping. That's when loyalties were really tested, and eventually some people caved and gave up Rider's name as not only an accomplice, but a man who'd been running the 'behind the scenes' for a lot of people for a long time." Sterling remembered the day Rider's name was announced on the news. Though he remembered Mel's horrified face as a reporter tried to get her to open up about her husband after a media ambush more. Now he fisted his hand against the thigh of his jeans.

"It might not have been such bad news had his bad deeds stopped there," Sterling continued. "But then it leaked that Rider had held Annie McHale in his basement for two days of her captivity, including the day the ransom video was recorded."

Marigold sucked in a breath.

"And I'm assuming Mel had no idea about it."

"None," he was quick to answer. "Though, since Annie and the missing FBI agent were never found, not everyone in town believes Mel. And of those who do believe that she had no idea, they blame her for having no idea about any of it. Annie, the corruption, everything wrong that Rider Partridge ever did during their one year of marriage. She was damned if she did, damned if she didn't."

Marigold took a moment to process that. Then, slowly, Sterling saw it.

Saw the question. If anyone else had asked him, he would have done what he always had before and become defensive, angry even.

But Marigold wasn't quick to blame, just curious.

"And you believed her? When she said she had no idea about what Rider was up to?"

Sterling picked up his hat and placed it on his head.

He was done with his coffee but stayed sitting long enough to answer.

"I've known Mel since we were teens. The only wrong thing she's ever done, in my opinion, was marry the wrong man."

That was all Marigold needed. He was glad to not have to spell out how Mel had become his closest friend after they'd met and kept the title long after they'd graduated. That he'd still been by her side when she'd started dating Rider and had been there for the marriage, too. Just as he had been at her side when he thought she needed him the most. Just as he had been with her up until the day she left him behind without a word.

Instead, Marigold let the conversation end and gave Sterling his space. It should have been time to go home, but he couldn't. Not yet. Not when he was still itching beneath the skin.

Sterling's feet instead led him to the sheriff's office.

Brutus Chamblin wasn't as jovial as he had been at Kenneth and Willa's wedding. In fact, he looked more than worn down.

"Before I tell you what's stuck in my craw, why don't you tell me what's stuck in yours?" Sterling used as a greeting.

Brutus had been at the department before Sterling had left it the first time around, but he hadn't been sheriff then. Maybe that's why he wasn't as formal as the title of sheriff deserved. Brutus didn't seem to mind. He waved a hand over some papers on his desk. One was the local paper, folded so Sterling couldn't see the main headline.

"The anniversary of Annie McHale's disappearance is coming up," Brutus started. "I've been told by the news editor that they plan to do an edition of the paper dedicated to everything that happened before, during and after The Flood. A 'very involved' piece."

Sterling whistled low.

"That's going to stir up some strong feelings," he decided on. "I just gave Marigold some bonus facts about The Flood, and it stirred up some feelings in *me*."

Brutus rubbed his chin.

"It surely will." He sighed. "This job as sheriff was supposed to be temporary, you know? I stepped in as interim sheriff because there was no one else. But can you even call me interim anything if I've been here for five years now?"

Sterling took a seat across from the older man. He rested his cowboy hat on his lap. Brutus's was on his desk already.

"You ever think about leaving? That'll force someone to step up. Or do you already have someone in mind for the job here?"

Brutus ran his thumb along his jaw.

"I've had a list for a while now but, as much as this department is changing, there's still a stench on the sheriff's office that everyone seems to smell. Can't blame good men and women for wanting a different path." He shrugged. "I almost didn't take the job myself, even when it was pitched to me as temporary."

He leaned back so far in his chair that Sterling thought he'd fall over. The older man cracked a smile. It wasn't amused, just something nice to do.

"There a reason you're here talking to my old bag of bones instead of doing something more fun?"

Sterling laughed.

"Well, I was going to come complain about how Kelby Creek doesn't let the past go, but, seems to me, we both might have had enough talk about that for today."

He stood and flipped his hat back onto his head. Brutus placed his hand on his own hat but didn't put it on.

Sterling didn't like how old he looked in the moment. He looked too worn.

"Maybe we both should go home and take a rest," Brutus finally said. "Would be nice to get some sleep finally."

He flashed a tired but genuine smile.

Sterling returned it.

"Might be nice," he agreed.

Brutus returned the sentiment.

"Might be nice."

MEL FELL ASLEEP in the guest room down the hall from the master bedroom. The cleaning crew had done a great job of keeping the interior of the house clean and dust-free. Mel even found that the sheets and linens smelled fresh, and she slept surprisingly well on them. Waking up, however, was a bumpier process.

Mel opened her eyes and knew she was drenched with sweat. She'd had a nightmare. It wasn't uncommon, but it wasn't exactly comfortable, either. She got out of bed and took her suitcase straight to the attached bathroom.

Mel cringed when she caught sight of her reflection in the mirror over the sink. The bandage had come off her forehead in her sleep and now she saw a nasty scab where she'd hit, she assumed, some part of her car. Along with her matted hair, thanks to the sweat, she looked worse for wear. Almost like she'd gotten drunk at a bar, tried to fight someone—and lost—and then had woken up with a hangover.

And that's how it felt, she decided as she got into the shower.

She felt just like she had a hangover. A nasty one at that. Her head hurt, with a tinge of fuzziness around it.

Was that how car accidents felt?

She hadn't been in one before.

"Rest, take it easy."

The doctor's voice echoed in her head. Mel resented that she could remember him clear as day but not why she'd been headed to Kelby Creek, of all places.

It was a dark, empty spot as if someone had hole-punched out her reason for wanting to be back and the actual drive in. Everything else was intact.

That frustration, plus her reflection when she got out of the shower put her already foul mood into another gear. She dressed quickly and started to snoop through the house slowly.

Surely there had to be a clue as to why she was there. Why she'd brought the house key with her, too.

Mel started with the second floor and went through the two guest bedrooms with precision. They, and the bathrooms, were stocked with typical guest bedroom things, just like the bathrooms. When she was done with them, she stopped at the door to the master suite.

She'd never understood why Rider had given the house to her in the divorce. His castle. His pride and joy. It had been just another reason why the town had suspected Mel of being involved in all the bad he'd done. It was also another reason why his brother, Jonathan, had been angry at her. He'd wanted the money that the sale could have gotten him had Rider decided to keep the house in his family.

Not let her have it.

Yet Mel hadn't sold the house. She hadn't lived in it after Rider had gone to prison, either.

It felt tainted.

It felt wrong.

It also was a reminder to everyone in Kelby Creek that with power came temptation and not everyone, when tempted, would resist.

It was also a reminder to Mel.

Ignorance was only bliss until that ignorance hurt someone else.

She turned the doorknob fast and walked inside the room with purpose.

The scream that came out of her mouth at what she saw echoed throughout the house.

Chapter Four

Sterling was rebellious.

He called Carlos, offered him a six-pack and asked if they could switch shifts. All before the sun had risen. Deputy Park was game, mostly because that's just who he was, but partially because Mel was coming in that morning for her statement and Carlos knew about their history.

That same history had kept Sterling up half the night.

"Switching shifts is no sweat off my back," Carlos had assured him. "I've been wanting to get Marigold's opinion on women anyways, so this is almost like a favor for me."

Sterling had thanked the man with a chuckle and then doubted his decision to let Carlos take Mel's statement and not him as soon as the phone call ended.

After that, he felt sure in his decision.

Then again, not so much.

That cycle continued on repeat before he forced his thoughts to turn to what he'd do instead of go into work.

Gym? Go for a run? Try to get a few hours of decent sleep?

Eventually Sterling decided to split the difference between all options.

He dressed in his gym clothes after the sun had risen and went to mow his lawn.

South Alabama had a habit of being a downright pain in the backside when it came to yard maintenance. You couldn't wait until the humidity or heat broke or else you'd be waiting on the porch watching your weeds grow and your grass turn brown. The only thing you could try to plan around was the rain. Sterling had one eye on the sky as he started his push mower at the curb.

The heat felt good and sweating felt better. Sterling's muscles got a workout, the grass got shorter and, dang sure enough, he was thinking about the first time he'd met Melanie Blankenship.

Sterling had been thirteen and as carefree as a kid could be. His brother, Sam, though, had been having issues. Other thirteen-year-olds had decided that, since Sam was a year younger, he needed picking on, something Sterling wouldn't have stood for, carefree or not. The bullies knew that and so they'd waited for Sam to be alone before picking on him. One day, they'd really been feeling themselves and let their words turn physical. They'd made Sam stand against the gym wall and pelted him with basketballs after practice.

Sterling had gotten the news through the grapevine and had run out of football practice and all the way to the gym, seeing red.

Yet the only person he'd seen getting beat up when he got there was Dan Leben.

The person throwing the punches was none other

than a girl half his size. Wearing braided pigtails and a sundress.

"You keep acting like a fool, Dan Leben, and I'll tell everyone that black eye you're going to have tomorrow came from a girl that's not even over five foot!"

Sterling had had a lot of memorable things happen to him in his life, but he'd never forget hearing Mel's little voice echo around the court.

He definitely wouldn't forget Dan listening to her, his cronies following him out, cussing like they were bad.

"Your brother's fine," Mel had assured Sterling when he'd run over. "He probably needs a bodyguard until he learns how to punch or run, though. Do you ride the bus or walk home?"

Sterling had been flustered at how she'd taken charge, but told her they rode their bikes. He'd told her where they'd lived, too, to which she'd shrugged.

"I live a few roads over, but I don't have a bike." She'd turned to Sam, who as a kid had already been quiet when attention wasn't directed at him. "I can walk you home, but you'll have to walk your bike. I have short legs."

To his surprise, Sam had agreed.

For the next three years, Mel had walked Sam home every day after school. The only reason she'd stopped was because she'd gotten her license. Then she drove him.

And when Sam had other plans or Mel's car broke down, Sterling was the one who did the driving.

Sterling finished mowing the lawn with a lot of guilt on his shoulders. This time not for the girl who stood up to bullies but for the kid being bullied.

He should have already told his brother that Mel was

back in town. He had been, at one time, the only other person Sterling knew who had cared about Mel with all that he had.

Sterling cut the ignition on the mower and wiped his arm along his brow. He didn't make it a step farther before someone was yelling at him.

"Hey there, cowboy!"

Sterling turned to see his neighbor, Ms. Martha, standing in his drive, her cordless phone waving in her hand. She had curlers tucked tight in her silver hair and was sporting a floral nightgown that was brighter than the sun. When she saw she had his attention, she added on to her greeting.

"Teddy Baker said there's a commotion going on at the sheriff's department," she called out. "I figured he might be lying, but if he wasn't then you might not know about it since you've been out here mowin'."

Sterling dropped his hands to his shorts and cussed low.

"I left my phone in the house," he realized.

Ms. Martha nodded.

"I thought you might've. Better go see if Teddy is a liar or just really good at gossipin'."

Sterling pulled his mower along to the garage while thanking the woman and was searching out his phone, all in under a minute flat.

He found the slick thing buried in his bed.

He had ten missed calls from several different numbers. All had left messages. He clicked on the earliest one.

It was from an unknown number, but the voice was unmistakable.

"Sterling, it's Mel. I—I need you to come over to the house as soon as possible." Her voice was shaking, but she didn't mince her next words. "I just found a woman in the bedroom—and, Sterling, someone killed her."

THE LAST TIME people in uniforms had swarmed the house, Rider Partridge had left in handcuffs. Behind him, a dazed and shaken Mel with tearstains on her cheeks and the guilt that she'd been nothing but blind. She'd watched him being escorted away by the FBI and the Dawn County Sheriff's Department. Those who were left, at least.

Sterling hadn't been there. Her world had decided to turn upside down while he'd been away with Sam and his father visiting his uncle.

Jonathan had been there, though. The fire hadn't happened yet, but he'd still been angry.

"Say something," he'd yelled at her. "Tell them they have it wrong. Tell them that your husband is innocent!"

But Mel's voice had already tried to convince the agents, and herself, that it was all a misunderstanding.

Then she'd finally gone into the basement. Then she'd seen the chair and rope.

On that front porch, she couldn't tell Jonathan anything. Definitely not that Rider was innocent.

Now it was the second time her house was swarming with uniforms. This time they were all from the sheriff's department.

And there was a body.

Mel was tucked away on the front porch. She was

careful not to get into foot traffic. She had her phone in her hand but had only made two calls.

"So you have no idea who the woman is." Detective Foster Lovett was smartly dressed and his badge professionally presented around his neck on a chain. His hair was long but groomed, and his wedding band glinted in the sun.

Mel shook her head. Again.

"Like I told Dispatch and Deputy Park, I didn't get the best look at her," she said. "As soon as I saw the blood and the—the—" She motioned to her chest and felt sick.

"—the gunshot wounds," he supplied.

"Yeah. After that I stopped looking altogether and called y'all."

Detective Lovett was taking notes.

"But you called Sterling Costner first, correct?"

His tone wasn't accusatory or judgmental. Just a man getting facts. Still, she smarted from the remark.

"To be honest, I don't have the best track record with people at the department," she responded. "I figured Deputy Costner wouldn't immediately point fingers at me, at the very least."

Mel wasn't sure if that was only reason she'd called him first, but she wasn't going to admit that.

"When he didn't answer, I called y'all. You can check my phone just like the last guy did."

Detective Lovett waved her off.

"I'm just getting a timeline here the best I can. If I were in your shoes, I might call a friend in the department first, too."

Mel nodded. The county CSI photographer walked out behind them. He'd been one of the first people to go in after Deputy Park had confirmed the body and secured Mel outside.

"I don't know how helpful I can be with all of this," she admitted before he could ask anything else. "Like I told Deputy Park, I'm not even sure why I'm in Kelby Creek."

Detective Lovett flipped his notebook closed. He put it in his back pocket.

"Head trauma is no joke. As for not remembering why you came here, you do know one thing even without having your memory."

Mel felt her eyebrow raise at that.

"And that is?"

"You made the decision within the last day and a half. So whatever prompted that decision now has a time frame. And it's a short one." He looked out at the street. Mel didn't follow his gaze. His demeanor changed ever so slightly from professional to tense. Then he sighed. "Regardless, once we've identified the body, we're going to have more questions for you. Excuse me a moment."

Mel didn't feel any comfort in his words but stepped aside and let him pass.

Had she recognized the woman lying across the bed that Mel had once called her own? No.

Had she looked hard?

No.

She'd seen the woman, the blood and the stillness, and she'd shut down.

Had the woman been there when Mel had come home the night before?

Just another question she didn't know the answer to, but that thought certainly sent a shiver down her spine.

Never mind the million-dollar one.

Who killed her?

Mel wrapped her arms around herself despite the heat. She finally turned to the growing crowd at the road. There she saw Detective Lovett talking to a newcomer.

Sterling's cowboy hat wasn't on, but he sure was sporting an official scowl. His brows were knitted together as he talked to the detective with fast words. He must have gotten her voice mail.

Mel expected those fast words to turn into fast walking toward her, yet the only direction Sterling walked was away. She lost sight of him a moment before he walked back up again. This time with the sheriff at his side.

Mel had known of Brutus Chamblin as a teen, but only because Sterling had been a fan of him.

"Dad said he's a good man and good people are hard to find," Sterling had told her the night he'd admitted he wanted to be a deputy. Sterling had been seventeen, but now Mel could see in the way he looked at the sheriff that that respect still burned just as bright.

They walked alongside each other and stopped at the top of the porch stairs.

"Ms. Blankenship." Sheriff Chamblin made it to her first. He stuck out his hand. Mel shook.

Sterling cut off any more introductions. His cool blue eyes were piercing as they met hers.

"Are you okay?" he asked.

"Yeah. Just a bit, well, shaken, I guess."

The sheriff nodded to that. He tapped Sterling's elbow.

"Understandable. How about you take a seat in one of these patio chairs and we'll be back down in a bit?"

Sterling's attention stuck to her only long enough for her to agree. Then both men disappeared into the house.

What felt like an hour went by, but Mel knew that logically it was more like twenty minutes before Sterling came back out. The sheriff had stayed behind, Detective Lovett and the coroner having been the only others to go into the house since then.

Sterling looked like he'd seen a ghost.

It gave her a deepening sense of dread.

"Other than the obvious, what's wrong?" Mel asked. "Wait. Did you recognize her? Do you know who the woman is?"

Sterling replied with a nod.

It was slow and ominous.

Mel hung on his every word as he answered.

"It's Rose Simon. She had her ID in her pocket."

"Rose Simon."

Mel chewed on the name for a second.

Then she understood Sterling's lead-in-the-belly look.

"Rose Simon, as in the reporter?" Sterling nodded. "As in the same woman who wrote the scathing investigative piece on Rider, which eventually helped lead to his conviction?"

Mel's mouth went dry.
Sterling's voice rumbled like thunder.
"The very same."

Chapter Five

He should have known the moment Cole Reiner came into the meeting room that everything private in his life was about to come to light.

"Hey there, Sterling. First time I've seen you in a while, huh?" Cole had become detective a year before and, as far as Sterling could guess, had been on several assignments that involved undercover work in and out of the county. Given his past—he'd once gone off everyone's radar to solve a mystery no one even knew existed—many people in the department called him an unofficial expert in that area of law enforcement work. Just as he was proving to be a skilled detective.

One who had come into the room with a notepad and pen to see Sterling.

Which couldn't be good.

"Can't say I'm excited to see you looking like you're about to read me my rights."

Cole waved him off and took a seat.

"If we were doing any of that, it wouldn't be me coming. Probably have Foster or Kenneth in here, all suits and stress lines turning into wrinkles. The only reason I'm really here is because there's some kind of kerfuffle at the hospital and everyone else is tied up at the crime scene." Sterling doubted that but didn't say as much. Cole smiled and motioned to himself. "So all you have is this pretty face to look at while I get some things straight."

He pressed the back of his pen and hovered it over his pad.

"Since I was out of pocket for a while, I'm going to need clarification on some things so we're all on the same page."

"And by *things* you mean me and Mel."

Cole nodded.

"If you listen to the gossip mill, it sounds like a simple scandal—Rider Partridge gets caught, arrested, convicted and goes to prison, then you and Mel shack up, become a thing, and then she skips town for 'insert an even more scandalous reason here.'" Cole raised his hand in defense quickly. "Let it be noted that while I listen to the gossip mill, I don't trust it. Once upon a time it said I was dead, so, for right now I'd rather you tell me the truth."

Sterling caught his bullhorn thoughts before they escaped his mouth. Then he settled.

He had known that there was a good chance someone would ask about him and Mel the moment a body had been found in her house.

A body connected to their pasts.

Sterling leaned back in his chair and felt naked without his hat.

"I grew up around Mel. Me, her and my brother,

Sam, were close," he started. "When Sam went to college, we became closer."

"Romantic?"

Sterling tensed at the feeling of someone prying but tried to calm himself again. Cole was a good guy and a better detective. Withholding any information from him, for whatever reason, wasn't a good idea.

Sterling shook his head.

"Not romantic, but there was something there that I was too stupid to see." Cole's eyebrow rose. Sterling simplified. "When Rider Partridge first asked Mel on a date, she came to me and asked if she should go. I encouraged her when I should have admitted I wanted to be with her. But, you know, young and dumb." Cole nodded in commiseration.

"Been there," he commented.

Sterling continued.

"I beat myself up for not doing anything for a while, but she seemed happy, and when they got married, I was already trying to move on." He sighed. "Then Rider was arrested and then convicted, and just like that, everyone turned on Mel like she was the monster in the suit."

"Not you."

Sterling shook his head.

"I went to visit her and found someone the world had worn down for no reason. When Rider was sent to prison and their divorce was final, I did the only thing that seemed right—I offered her a safe place to get her feet back under her. And that was it. I didn't want or expect anything more than that. Just a safe place with an old friend."

Cole put down his pen and nodded.

"But then something happened," he guessed.

Sterling nodded.

"One day she came out of her room and started talking, and it was like no time had passed from when we were kids to then. We got close and I finally told her what I should have when we were younger."

Sterling remembered the moment down to the smell of coffee and the sound of rain against the tin roof of his old house.

"I told her I loved her, and she said it back."

Cole took a moment. Smiled half that time before letting it slip.

"But then she left town."

Sterling felt himself tense. He nodded.

"No warning," he said. "A text that said to have a good life. The next time I saw her was at the hospital yesterday. I gave her a ride to the house."

There it was. The clarification of Sterling and Mel and what had happened five years ago.

It should have felt good to get it off his chest—to someone other than his brother and father—but it didn't. Sterling watched as Cole clicked his pen shut.

"That's rough. Any idea why she left?"

"None. And before you ask, no, I didn't ask yesterday. As far as I'm concerned, it doesn't matter."

That didn't feel entirely true, but Sterling stuck to his metaphorical guns.

"That's why you switched with Deputy Park today? So you wouldn't have to deal with all of that, I'm guessing."

"That's correct."

Cole nodded again, seemingly taking it all in. When he didn't try to get up and wave him on to leave, Sterling became suspicious.

"Am I a suspect in Rose's murder?" he asked.

Cole was quick to say no.

"Is Mel?"

It was something he knew would be questioned—Mel's innocence—but it hadn't occurred to him until then just how bad it probably looked.

Cole helped him see the big picture.

"Even if you take out her involvement with Rider, something is going on with her, Sterling." He leaned forward. "She comes back after five years, loses her memory of the last twenty-four hours or so and wakes up in a house she still owns for whatever reason that just so happens to have a dead body in it. The dead body of woman who, most could argue, put the final nail in the coffin of her husband's—and her—very posh life."

"Mel did not kill Rose." Of that Sterling was certain. Cole surprised him by nodding.

"That's true. She didn't. But that doesn't mean she didn't have something to do with it." Cole lowered his voice. "Sterling, Dr. Alvarez put Rose's time of death at almost a day ago. During the same time frame of Mel's missing memory. That could very well be a co-incidence, but it could just as easily mean something."

Sterling didn't like where this was going.

"So what are you saying? Is Mel under arrest?"

Cole straightened. He closed his notepad.

"No, but she's an extreme person of interest. And, Sterling, past or no past, I'd keep your distance until we get to the bottom of this." He stood but stayed severe. "Melanie Blankenship already broke your heart. Don't let her break the rest of your life, too."

THE ROOM SHE'D been questioned in was cold. The parking lot Mel walked out into afterward was hot. The difference made goose bumps erupt along her arm.

She looked for her car on reflex. It wasn't there, but Sterling was.

"Let's take a ride."

He was long-legged and handsome, leaning against his truck. Mel's stomach did a flip. She let out a breath. It shook a little.

"I don't think there's any place for me to go at the moment."

Sterling pushed off of the truck and opened the passenger's side door.

"I think I can help with that."

Sterling had them cruising away from the Dawn County Sheriff's Department without another word. He shut off the air-conditioning, rolled down the windows and slung one hand lazily on the steering wheel while the other rested outside the driver's side window.

Mel could almost forget she'd just been questioned about a murder.

Almost.

"Apparently if I hadn't had my accident, I'd be looking for a lawyer right now," she said after a moment. Mel turned her attention out her window. She didn't know where they were going, but at least the sun was out. "They said Rose was killed sometime between me being taken to the hospital and before I left. 'An airtight alibi.'"

She couldn't help but put some spice in her words at the last part. The sheriff had been the one to talk to her and, even though he'd been polite and professional, that phrasing had made her feel...guilty.

And she definitely hadn't killed Rose Simon. Memory or no memory.

By the sound of movement, Mel felt like Sterling nodded deep.

But "I heard" was all he said.

Mel glanced over at the man. He was still driving like they were back to being teens without much care in the world.

"He also asked about us," she said. "The sheriff, that is." Mel felt a warmth in her stomach turn to heat up her neck.

"He asked if we spent any time together last night after you gave me a ride."

Sterling shrugged.

"We didn't."

Mel felt her brow scrunch.

"Well, yeah, I know that. That's what I said."

Sterling nodded again.

The man who had once been fast to tell her exactly what was on his mind was giving her nods now.

Mel didn't like it. She tried again to get a reaction.

"I also had to explain, step by step, what I did when I got into the house," she said. "Including the fact that

I slept in the guest bedroom and didn't even go toward the master until I found her. I told him they can search and go through the house as much as they need. It definitely doesn't bother me."

There went the nod again, in sync with him turning them down a new street.

"Makes sense."

Mel couldn't take it anymore. She turned in her seat to face his profile.

"What's going on?" she asked, voice pitching a little high. "I mean, is this not talking to me because of what I did or is this not talking to me because you think I'm—what?—guilty of something? Because, even without my memory, I can assure you I haven't thought about Rose Simon or even known where she was in years and—"

They slowed down.

Mel cut herself off, recognizing the place they were approaching.

She stayed quiet as Sterling pulled in and put his truck in Park.

He had his door open and was out before Mel could say a word.

Then she watched him go into the gas station that had been around since before they were born. A few minutes later he was back, two familiar cups in his hand.

He handed her one through her window before going back to the driver's seat and settling in.

Mel looked down at the slushy in her hand. It was Coke flavored. Her favorite. She didn't need to look over at Sterling's to know his was blue raspberry. It helped that the gas station had only ever had the two flavors.

Sterling wordlessly drove them out of the parking lot and pointed them in a new direction.

Mel held her cup but didn't take a sip. Instead she waited as he turned off the paved street onto a dirt road. They bumped along it, the woods on one side and a field on the other.

The wind was warm against Mel's face. She also smelled rain, despite the clear sky. That and her cold hands around a slushy and Sterling at her side?

She was young and free.

No regrets, no broken heart, no decisions that altered anyone's lives.

She was just a girl sitting next to a boy, ready to waste some time doing nothing.

And that must have been the point.

Sterling turned onto a narrow dirt road that cut into the field before stopping at a section that had been turned into a patch where no grass or crops grew. A spot, they'd found, that had been long forgotten by Kelby Creek.

Sterling cut the engine and got out. Mel took a moment, then followed.

He was already sitting on his tailgate, sipping his slushy and looking out at the tall grass around them.

Mel followed suit.

Then they were both just sitting and sipping.

Just like they used to.

Sterling finally spoke after another few moments.

"Gayle Beecham and Brian Kingsley divorced a few months ago."

Mel turned her head so quickly she could have sworn she heard a snap.

"What? Really?"

He moved his straw around in his drink.

"Yep. And you'll never guess why."

Mel leaned in. Sterling smirked.

"Don't tell me it's because of her sister."

He nodded.

"Yes, ma'am. Turns out we were right. Brian was head over heels for Lydia Beecham this whole time."

That was some gossip Mel hadn't heard. Not that she'd heard any from Kelby Creek since she'd left.

"Ask me who Brian is married to now," Sterling added.

Mel hit his shoulder, mouth agape.

"No way," she squealed. "Don't tell me Brian and Lydia already took that step!"

Sterling laughed.

"They did a courthouse thing, and ten guesses as to who their witness was."

Mel was absolutely stunned.

"If you say Gayle, I will lose it."

Sterling held his hands up in defense and shrugged.

"Then I won't say it."

Mel laughed and slapped at his shoulder again.

"That's either very understanding of her or one heck of a power move," he said. "But, as far as I know, no one has had the courage to ask."

He joined in with his own laughter when Mel couldn't help but keep it up.

It felt nice. Not only to laugh and really mean it, but to do it with him again.

Just catching up.

Because she'd been gone for five years with no contact with anyone, especially him.

Mel let her amusement die down.

The condensation on the side of her cup wet her hands.

She kept her eyes on the distance.

A breeze pressed against them before going on its way.

They could only pretend for so long that everyone was okay.

Mel let out a long, low breath.

"Kelby Creek has a wound." Her voice was quiet, but she knew Sterling could hear her perfectly. "The Flood opened it, and I'm not sure if it can ever really close. Not completely and not without leaving a nasty scar if it did. When you have a wound like that, a scar like that, you become more aware of what made it." She put her cup down and grabbed onto the tailgate, palms down to give her more stability as she leaned forward to talk into the heat. "I'm a reminder. A walking, talking reminder that not all wounds are made by weapons and bad people. Sometimes they're made by people trying to pretend that everything is okay."

She looked at Sterling. He was already staring. There was no trace of humor in his expression, either.

Mel laid out her point.

"I never knew to stop Rider, but I do know how to stop being a constant reminder of him. Sterling, I never planned on coming back to Kelby Creek. Never."

Sterling's jaw set.

Birds chirped in the distance. That smell of rain seemed to become stronger.

When Sterling responded, his voice was hard.

"Then let's figure out why you're back and how Rose Simon is connected," he said, resolute. "After that, you can go again and never look back."

It was what Mel wanted, yet, she felt hesitation at the words.

Sterling's cool blue eyes bit into her.

She almost told him then—the real reason why she'd left town the way she had—but instead she nodded.

If Sterling knew Rider's last words to her before he'd gone to prison, he'd do something heroic.

And one thing Rider had proven to be very skilled at?

Destroying heroes.

So Mel kept her mouth shut and they finished their drinks in silence.

They didn't see the big picture yet. Or, if Melanie Blankenship was telling the truth, at least one of them didn't remember it.

She straightened her ball cap and looked at the dirt road Melanie and Sterling had driven across minutes ago.

She was waiting, but she didn't know for what yet. Whatever it was, it wasn't going to be good.

Not after the car accident with Melanie.

Definitely not after Rose's murder.

She cussed low and kicked a stick out of the tree line. Her phone rang shortly after.

She ignored the call.

If Melanie truly didn't remember why she'd come back to town, she definitely didn't remember that it was her who was supposed to be dead in that bedroom.

Not Rose.

She waited a few seconds more, then went back into the woods.

Chapter Six

They went to the accident site first. Sterling watched as Mel gingerly picked through the dirt on the shoulder of the road before combing the area for a fifth time.

He was right there with her.

Neither found anything useful, and no memories surfaced.

Then the rain came and with it a new sense of urgency. It didn't help that they were back at the house they'd been so quick to leave that morning.

"And you're sure there's nothing in there that we will mess up?" Mel peered through the windshield at the front porch. To prove his earlier point of telling her that they could go inside, he pulled away from the curb and drove up to park in the drive.

"Foster said they just all cleared out. We're good to go in."

Mel didn't seem so sure, but the rain had followed them and it was enough to get her moving. They were soon in the grand, slightly ridiculous foyer.

It echoed.

Sterling hated it.

He also wasn't a fan of his phone at the moment. It vibrated with anger.

"And now it looks like we're under a tornado watch." He snorted. "The cherry on top of the day, huh?"

Mel was barely listening. Her eyes were trained on the stairs. Sterling softened.

"We don't have to be here right now," he reminded her. "This place has been checked from top to bottom and nothing came of it."

Mel was insistent. She waved off his concern.

"This is technically my house, so this is my responsibility. At the very least I can not be a coward and pay it the same attention as where I had the accident."

She moved fast up the stairs. Sterling used his long legs to outwalk her. While he'd stood by as the house was being searched and secured several times over that morning, nothing changed the fact that a woman had been murdered there.

So he led the way to the open door of the master bedroom. The bed was bare, linens stripped, but there was a spot on the mattress.

A dark, angry one.

Mel made a noise when she saw it. Out of reflex he reached out and touched her back to steady her.

"That—that's blood," she realized.

"That's something I can take care of when the rain stops," he said. "That's also something you don't need to look at now."

Mel shook her head and stepped into the room. Sterling watched as her face hardened. She didn't say anything as she started to move around the room, searching for something that might help her make sense of everything.

He wished it could be that simple.

After a few minutes, they both admitted defeat.

Mel next showed him to the guest bedroom where she'd spent the night. Her bag was open, but her things weren't thrown around.

"That's nice at least," she mused. "They were gentle with my unmentionables."

Sterling walked over to the suitcase and knocked on the hard top.

"What *did* you pack for your trip here? Any clue in that?"

"Nope. Just clothes, basic toiletries and a phone charger. My emergency makeup made the trip, but that's because I always have it packed."

Sterling motioned to the case.

"Can I look?"

Mel nodded.

"I don't know what you think you'll find. Me and the detectives went through it already."

Sterling wasn't put off by her skepticism.

"Well, what about your actual clothes?"

"What?"

Sterling pulled out a pair of shorts, jeans and a blouse. He didn't take any of her underthings out, but he did note them.

"Unless something has changed, I'm assuming you weren't coming to town for a romantic tryst." Mel's eyes widened. Her cheeks tinted to a rosy shade. "If you had,

I think you would have packed some frilly numbers instead of your sensible ones."

"My sensible ones?" She laughed despite her face becoming the color of a cherry. "Sterling. Are you talking about my underwear?"

He shrugged.

"You wear the frilly, lacy things in the beginning of a relationship but the sensible, comfortable ones when *you're* comfortable." He waved his hand over her suitcase. "I only saw the comfortable ones. Though, to be honest, I always liked those better."

Sterling hadn't meant to say the last part, but it was true. Remembering her walking around the house in his T-shirt and her black cotton panties had been a sight worth seeing.

"So unless you were meeting someone here who you've already been dating awhile, I'm going to go out on a limb and say that your reasons for being here in Kelby Creek are not romantic in nature."

Mel looked like she might disagree with his guess but surprised him with another laugh. This one had some bitterness to it.

"The only long-term relationship I'm in at the moment is with an amazing boss who was kind enough not to fire me when I called her claiming amnesia and asked for a few days."

Sterling felt some relief at her answer, even though he shouldn't have.

"That's the first I've heard you talk about work," he said, spreading out the rest of her clothes on the bed.

He recognized every piece but one. "What did you end up doing?"

At this, Mel seemed to tuck in on herself. Like she was timid.

Sterling felt his eyebrow raise.

"Don't tell me you went into some big corporate job or something stock-related." It was something Rider had pushed on her when they'd been dating. A directive that he had probably been hoping would lead to Mel being his accomplice.

Now she shook her head.

"I—uh—write for a home decor magazine."

Sterling felt his brow rise as high as it could but not because he was surprised at the choice. But because it had been a dream of hers since they were kids...and she seemed ashamed of it.

"Mel, that's great. Isn't it?"

She shrugged.

"It's not like I work for the great *Southern Living* magazine."

"But there can be more than one great thing out there. Do you like the work?"

This time there was no shame. Mel nodded.

"I do. It's an up-and-coming magazine, too, so I've been able to see it grow from the ground up."

There it was.

A genuine Melanie Blankenship smile.

Normally, it would have made him happy to see her truly care about something.

But, in that moment, it was a reminder.

A reminder that he'd missed out on the last five years of her life.

Or, more aptly, he'd been left out of those five years on purpose.

It sobered Sterling.

He cleared his throat and put his attention back on the clothing lined up across the bed.

"It looks like you packed for comfort and functionality instead of flashy or official. For the most part." He pointed to the dress. It was slate gray with black trim and a belt. It gave the impression of being severe among the other laid-back outfits.

In other words, it didn't fit.

Mel took a step closer. Her shoulder brushed his arm. He kept his attention, however, on her expression.

It, coupled with a slight head tilt to the side, let Sterling know he was onto something before she even said a word.

"It's my interview dress," she stated simply. Mel picked it up, looking at it like it was brand-new.

"Your interview dress?"

"Yeah. I wanted to get an interview outfit that would help people take me more seriously since, well, since sometimes my height makes me look like a child." She shook the dress a little. "I put this puppy on and got my current job. My boss even told me after that I had looked almost intimidating—like I meant business and that she needed to listen to *me*. I'm pretty sure she was just joking, but that always stuck with me. It also has pockets, which is a bonus."

As she spoke, Mel slid her hands into said pockets. At the second one she made a noise.

Then she pulled out a piece of paper.

It was small and folded tight.

Sterling moved closer. He bent over a little while she opened it.

Mel smelled like lavender.

He recognized her handwriting, scrawled across the paper when it was laid flat.

"It's an address. One twenty-four Locklear Lane. I—I don't know where that is off the top of my head."

Sterling felt the tension line his shoulders. Mel looked up at him. He knew he had blue eyes, but hers were on another planet. They pierced right through him every time.

"Do you know it?"

Sterling nodded.

"It's in Kelby Creek."

Excitement filled those nearly gray eyes.

"This could be why I came back, then!"

Sterling didn't share in her joy at having a potential answer.

Especially since he knew exactly where that was.

He took the paper from her hands to make sure he was reading it right.

He was.

"I really hope it isn't."

ONE TWENTY-FOUR Locklear Lane had seen much better days. One of three houses along the street, it was on the far side of town, a cool five-minute walk from the county line. An empty lot stretched behind 124 and had weeds so grown-up that no mower would be able to deal with them without help.

Mel got out of Sterling's truck and did something really unladylike.

She swore low and plenty.

"I never knew the actual address," she said after. "I only came here once with the FBI."

Sterling walked up, a flashlight in his hand.

The rain had let up, but the sky was still dark.

It made the house in the distance feel even more ominous.

Mel glanced up at him, trying to read his face.

He had it closed down, but his words carried enough weight.

"Mark Raynard's house. Aka where our corrupt sheriff met with our corrupt mayor to hash out the details on how they'd go about kidnapping and ransoming Annie McHale."

"The very same house they believe Annie McHale was taken to after being tied up in mine."

Thunder rumbled in the distance.

It fit the mood.

"I haven't thought about this place in years. Why would I have written the address down? Why would I have wanted to come here?"

Sterling clicked on the flashlight.

"The only way to get answers is to go forward. But if we see anything suspicious, we're calling someone."

Mel nodded and followed as Sterling led them up a

cracked and crumbling sidewalk. The porch wasn't in better shape.

"The bank took possession of this place a few years back," Sterling said, picking up on her thoughts. "They were supposed to renovate it and try to sell it but, for whatever reason, no one has touched it. Rumor is Annie McHale's parents actually bought it on the down low, though, since it was such a big part of the investigation. Regardless, no one has lived here since The Flood."

The front door was locked and so was the back door. The window at the back that led into the kitchen, however, was unlocked. Sterling slid it open with ease. What he couldn't do with ease was climb inside.

"Sometimes being as big as a mountain has its drawbacks," he joked.

Mel rolled her eyes and took the flashlight.

"And sometimes being as small as a preteen has its advantages."

Sterling hesitated.

Mel put her hands on her hips.

"We need some answers. If this house has to do with why I came to Kelby Creek, then I need to see inside it. Plus, it's clearly not in use. What's the worst that can happen?" Sterling gave her a long look. "Okay, not the smartest thing to say, considering," she admitted. "But I'm going inside the house whether you like it or not. So please, Mountain Man, give me a boost so we can get this over with faster."

It was Sterling's turn to roll his eyes.

"I feel like we're back at Tina Lowell's eighteenth birthday party again."

That made Mel chuckle.

"Except this time we're not trying to escape a weird, rave-like party through a bathroom window because we're too chicken to tell Tina that her college friends are freaking us out."

"I wasn't chicken," he pointed out, turning her around with his hand. Mel felt rosier for it. "I just didn't want to have to deal with watching Sam trying to be overly polite about it. He sure takes care not to hurt anyone's feelings."

Mel felt a stab to her chest at the mention of Sterling's brother. While they hadn't talked much about their time apart, or her leaving the way she did, they certainly hadn't touched once on Sam. Because, as much as she'd hated it, she hadn't just cut off Sterling. She hadn't spoken to Sam since the day she left. It hurt. That pain, that action, hadn't been brought up yet by Sterling, though, surprising her. She wondered if he'd been skirting it on purpose.

"Just unlock the door when you get in," Sterling continued, voice changing to nothing but focus. "Don't go looking around first. Okay?"

"Aye-aye, Deputy."

Sterling hoisted her up and through the opening like she was a feather. If she wasn't doing her own mental focusing, she might have taken a moment to marvel at how, after all these years, it felt good to have his hands on her.

How easy it felt to be together.

But now wasn't the time.

Mel climbed down from the countertop beneath the

window and scanned her new surroundings. Unlike her house, abandoned yet still kept, this one looked like a haunted house that hadn't seen a human since the '80s.

It smelled stale and of mold, and dust coated every available surface left behind in the kitchen. When Mel was upright, she wiped the dust from the counter from her hands onto her jeans. On cue, she sneezed.

She never saw the man coming.

Chapter Seven

The baseball bat made a crack against the floor. Mel fell back with a scream. Her elbows hit the counter right before her back collided with the wood.

The man, wrapped in a dark gray hoodie that helped block his face from view, didn't bring the bat back up. Instead he took the stance of a golfer and swung it across the floor.

Right at Mel.

She scrambled to the side but felt the wind from the swing. The bat hit the cabinet next to her. It was so fast and loud Mel didn't have the time to figure out how to avoid the next hit.

The man lifted the bat high.

He never brought it back down.

The back door was off its hinges in an explosion of force and wood.

Sterling was a man enraged.

The man in the hoodie tried to redirect his swing, but Sterling wasn't having it. He caught the bat by its end, halting the swing. He refused to give it up.

Something the man must have felt in the power of

the hold. He must have also decided then that a hand-to-hand with Sterling wasn't in his best interest.

The man let go of his weapon and ran deeper into the house within a second flat. Sterling gave her a quick look.

She was fine, scared but unhurt.

He didn't need to protect her now.

He needed to stop the man who'd tried to hurt her instead.

The bat hit the floor as he took off to the next room.

Mel scuttled toward the bat and scooped it up without getting to her feet. Adrenaline made her hands shake; confusion and shock kept her quiet.

That didn't last long, though. The sound of an impact came from the front of the house, followed by glass shattering.

Mel got to her feet, bat clutched in her hands. She moved to the adjoining room, heart in her throat.

The former dining room was small and empty. It gave her an easy view of the living room that came next. There she saw Sterling struggling to his feet in front of a large broken window.

She hurried forward.

"Oh my God, Sterling, are you—"

Mel saw the blood across his lip, but she didn't see the bullet that broke the last living room window next to her.

She certainly heard it, though.

Chaos, loud and violent, broke out. Sterling was yelling right along with it. He threw his weight against her. Another bullet hit somewhere above them.

They met the ground so quickly that the air pushed out of Mel's lungs. She convulsed into a coughing fit as Sterling's body became a cage around her.

The two shots turned into several more. Mel would have screamed if she could have. Instead she held on to the bat and closed her eyes tight.

When the world quieted down, her ears still rang.

"Come on!"

Two large hands wrapped around her side. Sterling moved Mel as effortlessly as he had boosted her into and through the window. One second she was on the living room floor; the next Sterling was pressing her against the hardwood of the old dining room.

"Stay down," he growled at her.

She wasn't about to do anything else.

Gunfire erupted behind them again. At least now there were two walls between them and the outside.

"How is he doing this?"

The words left Mel's mouth in a jumble of sound and fear. She meant to ask how one man was causing so much damage, but all her thoughts got tangled up together.

It didn't help when the second break of gunfire happened and Sterling pushed her across the floor, closer to the wall, his own gun now in hand.

"Stay down," he said, voice so low it seemed to thrum against her hammering heart.

"You can't—" she started, but Sterling was already out of the room.

Mel waited to hear more shots, but nothing happened. The silence felt infinite. She was too afraid to move—to make a sound. All she had was questions and fear.

Who was the man?

Why was he here?

And why wouldn't he just leave?

Glass crunched in the living room. Mel tensed, worried their unknown gunman had come back, but it was Sterling who appeared through the doorway.

His look of determination and focus had transformed.

He looked nervous.

Which definitely wasn't good news for them.

"We need to move. Now."

His words were rushed. He hooked a hand under her elbow and lifted her up in one fell swoop.

"Did he leave?" Mel asked, stumbling against him. She kept the bat clutched against her chest.

Instead of going out through the now-broken back door, Sterling turned them to a small hallway connecting to the other side of the house. He hesitated between two open doors before shutting the one on the left.

He pushed her through the door on the right.

"The attic access is in here." He opened the bedroom's closet door, and sure enough, the access door was in the ceiling. It was one panel and a small opening.

"Why do we need the attic access?"

"Because I'm pretty sure our gunman brought friends."

The ceiling was low enough that Sterling was able to use his height to split the difference. His fingertips touched the panel, and he jumped. It moved and slid to the side.

Then he turned to Mel.

"I need you to hide."

He didn't leave room for discussion. Sterling hoisted her up and lifted her until her hands found the edge of the access. She didn't need to struggle to get herself all the way up. Sterling used his strength, and her backside, to make the trip an easy one.

The attic was dark—horror-movie dark. When Sterling passed her the baseball bat, she held on to it for dear life.

"Call the department." Sterling was still talking low. He was fast when he tossed her his phone. Thankfully, she caught it one-handed.

Even if that hand was shaking.

"Two cars pulled up. One confirmed shooter."

Mel shook her head.

"Get up here with me." But she knew already that he wasn't going to.

No.

Sterling was going to fight back to keep her safe.

Just like he always had.

Something crashed on the other side of the house.

"Close the door," he repeated.

Mel watched helplessly as he drew his gun.

She hesitated.

Then she closed the door.

The darkness consumed her.

If HE COULD HAVE, Sterling would have made a series of different choices leading up to his current predicament.

The first decision Sterling would have corrected

would have been coming to 124 Locklear Lane with Mel in tow. He simply wouldn't have.

Aside from that blaring fact, he should have called in Foster or the sheriff from the get-go. Hell, he should have called in Cole Reiner since Mel had already landed on his, and everyone else's, radar.

But Sterling hadn't.

Mainly because of what Cole had said about Mel breaking his life.

Sterling had felt defensive of the woman. And the implication that Mel might be malicious.

Even if the first part had been right on the money.

Mel *had* broken his heart. He wasn't above admitting that to himself, even if it took some nudging to admit it out loud.

But Mel breaking his life?

Well, he didn't like anyone thinking she could or would do that to someone.

Not again.

Not because of him.

So, maybe a part of Sterling had kept from telling anyone about their plans because he had wanted to prove that Mel had found herself in someone else's trouble, not her own.

Then there was also the fact that he hadn't actually thought they'd find anything.

What *could* they find there after all these years?

Regardless of any answer, it was a bad call on his part.

Another choice he would have liked to change, had he had the power, was where he'd parked his truck.

It was at the curb. Not in the drive. Had he parked it at the end of the concrete pad, running to it from the back door might not have been that far-fetched a plan.

But now it was an impossibility.

After he'd gone to the window to get a bead on the gunman, he'd seen something no one needed during a fight.

More numbers for the opposing side.

Two cars pulled up, and the gunman ran right up to one without hesitation.

Now, assuming the two new arrivals were associated with their unknown attacker, running out to the road *behind* their vehicles was an absolute no.

The last regret Sterling would have loved to correct?

He wished he'd worn his uniform, not his street clothes, and therefore had all the bells and whistles that came with it. Not just his service weapon and his badge in his back pocket.

Sterling hung inside the bedroom long enough to hear Mel slide the attic access panel door over. Whatever noise had sounded from the front of the house had turned to footsteps.

Sterling took a deep breath and steadied the weight of the gun in his hand.

One twenty-four Locklear Lane was known to most locals of Kelby Creek as the Meeting House. It had garnered the nickname thanks to the corrupt mayor and sheriff holding their clandestine dealings there. But only after The Flood had almost drowned the whole town. The homeowner eventually was suspected when the testimony of a sheriff's deputy in exchange for a lighter sentence led the FBI back to him and the house.

From there the FBI had pulled on that thread until it had connected to Rider Partridge. That was why Sterling didn't know as much about the layout of the actual house as what had happened inside its walls.

Now it was just another regret.

Especially when a man appeared at the opposite end of the hallway that Sterling didn't know even connected to the front of the house.

He was tall and looked like he was built tough. The man was in a T-shirt and jeans. His belt buckle was thick and had a shining Harley-Davidson logo on it. There was an empty holster next to it.

He wasn't the man in the hoodie but seemed as ready to rumble as their first attacker.

He had a gun in his hand.

Sterling opened his mouth to identify himself, but the man pulled his weapon up.

So Sterling shot.

Several things happened at once after that.

The man took the bullet to the shoulder, a sickening sound of impact and pain, just as he let off a round. It burrowed into the wall right next to Sterling's head. His eardrums rang, but he didn't stumble.

Sterling was ready to take a second shot, disabling the man so he could take his gun, when another absolute shock of the day did him in.

Another fighter entered the metaphorical ring through the doorway that led into the kitchen.

This time, it was a woman with blond hair, wearing

a ball cap and large sunglasses, and decked out in all black. She wasn't that tall, but what she had, other than the element of surprise, was enough.

She rammed into Sterling, hands out. It caught him off guard, and he went back. He connected with the hallway wall. The woman grabbed at his arm holding the gun. The man at the other end of the walkway could have used the moment as an opening to shoot Sterling.

But he didn't.

He clutched at his wound and ran.

The woman did not.

She was fast and nimble, grabbing at his wrist while throwing a knee to his groin.

Sterling couldn't help the noise he made at the new burst of pain. He also couldn't let go of the gun.

It was Sterling's turn to check the woman. He created space between them with a hard hit of his shoulder against her arm. When that space was enough for him to bring his gun around, Sterling heard something he definitely didn't want to hear.

A man, he wasn't sure which one, yelled out.

"Where is she?"

It pulled both his attention away, as well as that of the woman he was fighting.

"Check the bedrooms," yelled another man.

Footsteps came closer to the other end of the hallway.

The woman didn't blink at the new directives being given. Instead she tried another groin kick. Sterling moved just in time to block. Then he had the room to bring his gun up.

The woman froze.

Just as the man who'd been shot came back into view.

"I'll shoot," Sterling growled, warning the man.

While also hoping they were together. If not, the only leverage Sterling had would be gone and there would be nothing stopping the other man from shooting him right then and there.

Luckily, it seemed they were together.

The man kept his gun aimed but didn't shoot.

"Dawn County Sheriff's Department," Sterling finally was able to say. "Lower your weapon."

Movement behind the woman let Sterling know that his decision to step into the small hallway was another thing to add to his regrets list.

The man in the hoodie appeared over the woman's shoulder.

He had his gun raised, too.

Sterling had no place to go.

"You lower your weapon," Hoodie demanded.

Sterling glanced at the man to his left. He wasn't moving, and without the woman, Sterling was as good as shot.

"Tell your man down there to lower his," he replied.

Hoodie shook his head.

"We both know he's keeping you in check. He stays. But she leaves."

He nodded to the woman.

Sterling could see his reflection in her too-big sunglasses.

"You can get out of this, Deputy," Hoodie added. "Let her go, drop your gun and then we go. Simple."

"Considering both of you have already shot at me, I'm not inclined—"

Sterling stopped talking the moment he heard something new.

Sirens.

Unmistakable and close.

Cruiser sirens.

Hoodie's eyes widened. His entire demeanor changed.

Sterling knew then what would happen next.

Hoodie had made a decision. One that involved blood.

Hoodie's finger moved in sync with Sterling's aim.

Neither had the time to worry about the man at the end of the hallway.

Not when they were about to shoot each other.

Those sirens got louder. Sterling braced for the impact of the other shooter. The woman tensed.

Then the ceiling exploded in a series of bangs. Like someone was hitting it with something hard.

Three people in that hallway and doorway looked up, surprised.

Sterling didn't.

Instead, he pulled the trigger.

Chapter Eight

Mel lifted the bat as soon as the shooting started. She stumbled back into the darkness of the attic. Her foot missed the wooden beam. She tripped trying to catch herself and landed hard on the plywood that made up the ceiling.

Had it been a newer house she might have crashed through the ceiling to the hallway below, but this house was older and built like a beast. All she did was make an awful thud noise, mixed in with her small yell of surprise.

It must have been louder than she'd thought.

A man's voice boomed beneath her.

Then a shot came through the floor.

Mel screamed, getting to her feet as light came through a hole near her.

She didn't wait to assess the damage.

Mel did her best to run back in the direction of the bedroom she'd been above.

She went the wrong way.

Her foot found air instead of wood. She nose-dived forward from her momentum.

Mel must have found the one part of the Meeting House that wasn't built to last. Whether it was water damage, the ravages of neglect or some small crack she hit just right, Mel went from falling to the floor to crashing through it.

Like a scared animal, she scrambled to grab on to something. All she managed in the end was to shield her face with one of her forearms.

Pain and several other sensations she couldn't grab on to followed her from the darkness to the light of the room below.

The leg of her jeans snagged on something just as a scream tore out of her mouth. It was enough to jolt new pain through her. It also kept her from crashing face-first into the wooden floor below. Debris from the ceiling hit the ground while she stopped and swung a few feet off the floor.

Mel's hair reached downward; her blouse went over to expose her stomach.

Through it all, Mel realized she still had the bat in one hand.

Which was good, since the person who was gawking at her from the doorway wasn't a handsome deputy she knew.

A man she hadn't seen before was clutching his shoulder with one hand and pressing into his stomach with the other. Blood had thoroughly stained his T-shirt.

Mel wasn't about to ask questions.

She tried to swing out, making a strangled sound in the process. All the motion did was start to dislodge her. Her jeans ripped. Finally she dropped the bat. The man ran. Mel tried to focus on minimizing her fall by putting her arms out, but there was no time.

Her jeans were done holding her weight. The tension keeping her in the air broke, and Mel fell straight down.

It was a good thing Sterling was faster. His arms were around her waist, stopping the fall inches from her head meeting the floor.

"I got you," he grunted.

"The man—" Mel started, but Sterling twirled her around like she was a rag doll, shaking his head.

"Trust me. He's not getting far."

Mel let herself be righted by the cowboy deputy.

"What about the other man?"

Sterling studied her. His eyes were narrowed, focused. There was blood on his lip. He was sweating and breathing hard.

The sounds of sirens and squealing tires outside filled the house.

Sterling tucked her into his side, arm around her hip and hand fastened tight.

He didn't move.

"I'm only worrying about you right now."

Mel could have gone the rest of her life without seeing the inside of the Dawn County Sheriff's Department again and been happier for it. Yet, there she was staring at its beige walls and scuffed tile floors for a second time that day.

At least now she was in an open room with windows and a coffee in hand instead of one with only a metal table and the distinct feeling of being judged.

She also wasn't waiting alone.

Sterling was in a mood, rightfully so.

He'd somehow acquired a cowboy hat she didn't recognize and a scowl she did.

He was angry and trying his damnedest to keep it from spilling out. It made the man uncharacteristically quiet. He hadn't even said much on the ride over, though that might have been because he was in some pain.

Under the fluorescent lights of the sheriff's department's meeting room, his wounds looked worse than they had fresh. His lip was busted, and there was a decent bruise ringing his left eye. Mel also suspected there was some bruising beneath his clothes, but he wasn't going to admit that to her. Not when he was like this.

Not when he thought they'd lost.

And that's what had happened, in so many ways.

They'd walked into something and had barely walked out of it.

Mel drank a long pull of her coffee.

"It would be nice if my memory would come back. Even just a little."

Sterling moved his gaze from the whiteboard at the end of the room to Mel.

A thousand-mile stare had his blue eyes trapped somewhere else.

Mel put down her cup and tried to think of something to say to get her past the feeling of discomfort and lingering fear. Something he would respond to— something that would break the barrier that had shot up around him since the attack.

That something never came to mind.

Cole Reiner, however, bustled into the room with a folder beneath his arm, papers in his hand and a pen held between his teeth.

"Sorry," he said around it. "A lot going on."

Detective Reiner dropped down into the seat at the head of the table. The papers and folder hit the table; the pen went on top.

He was red in the face, but she couldn't tell if that was from frustration or sunburn. Mel might have been a local, and she might have had a more intimate knowledge of the inner workings of what had taken place during The Flood, but Cole was largely a stranger to her. The only reason she trusted him was because Sterling did.

Sterling turned in his chair, opening his body language to the man. His voice came out gruff.

"Please tell me you got them."

Detective Reiner shook his head. Sterling cussed low.

"Our mystery blonde and the hooded gunman are in the proverbial wind," Reiner said with notable frustration. "But everyone in Dawn County, the neighboring county and the city police department are looking. We've even activated our reserve deputies. They're limited in number but highly motivated in their work." Reiner clasped his hands together and leaned over onto the table. His expression went from focused to determined, tinged with anger. "They attacked one of our own, and that's not something we take lightly. We'll find them."

Sterling nodded and rolled back his shoulders.

Mel wished she could help. Wished she had the

magic answer to whom the people at that house had been, but she didn't. She didn't even know why the paper with the address had been in her dress pocket.

"What about the other man?" she piped in. "The one who was shot."

Reiner glanced at Sterling. Neither was quick to answer.

Which meant it wasn't good.

"He's in surgery," Reiner supplied after a moment. "We're still trying to identify him, since the doctors aren't confident he'll survive the night."

That should have given her some kind of relief—the man who had attacked and shot at Sterling wouldn't be able to do it again—but Mel just felt frustration.

"I still don't understand why they were even there." She balled her fist on top of the table. It was cool against her skin. "I don't understand why *we* were there. Why did I write the address down?"

It was a repeating rhetorical question that Mel didn't expect anyone to answer.

Yet Reiner perked up.

Though it didn't seem like he was waiting to tell them good news.

"That's something I wanted to talk to you about." Reiner looked directly at her. Sterling tensed in his chair. Mel's stomach joined in. Reiner produced a picture from the stack of papers beneath his hands. He didn't slide it over right away.

"Rose Simon's murder was placed at around one thirty yesterday," Reiner continued. "And it occurred somewhere other than your residence. We're still look-

ing for the where, but now we have the how." He looked
at Sterling for this answer. "The gun you got away
from your attacker had bullets that matched the ones
recovered from Rose. Same make and caliber. Even
matching marks on the bullet left by the scraping of
the old gun."

Sterling took off his cowboy hat and rubbed a hand
along his jaw.

He didn't say anything. Maybe because he knew that
wasn't all.

Reiner's gaze swung back to her. This time he did
slide something over.

It was a picture of a car that had seen better days.
The bumper was crunched, and the windshield had a
crack running through it. One headlight was broken.

Mel didn't recognize it.

She said as much.

"Whose is it?"

Reiner searched her face. He must have decided what
he saw was what he needed. His voice was low.

"Rose Simon's." Sterling took the picture. He shared
a questioning look with Reiner before the detective nodded.

"What?" Mel asked. "What is it?"

Sterling sighed.

"This is the other car from your accident yesterday,"
he answered. "This is the car that hit you and ran. We
found it parked outside the Kintucket Woods. Consis-
tent damage with your vehicle."

Mel stood and reached way over to grab the picture back.

"Rose hit me?" She searched the picture with new understanding.

It did no good.

"I just don't get it," she continued. "I come back to Kelby Creek with the Meeting House address in my pocket, am run off the road by Rose Simon, who is then killed by a man I don't know before being placed in my old bedroom? Then we run into that same man at the Meeting House, plus two other people I don't know?"

Mel sat heavily back into her chair.

Tears of frustration started to prick the corners of her eyes.

"It all sounds like some kind of a bad dream," she added. "Sunday morning I was drinking coffee in my apartment, happy to finish an article about high-end patio furniture, and two days later I'm in the middle of *this*. I don't understand."

Mel fisted her hands on top of the table again.

Sterling was the first to speak, but only after he shared one more look with the detective.

Mel realized then that she was missing a piece of the story.

And she probably wasn't going to like that piece.

"I'm not so sure you're in the middle of it," Sterling started. "I actually think you're the point of it."

"What do you mean?"

Mel felt her eyebrow raise just as her stomach dropped. Sterling now looked mad.

"At the Meeting House, before you put up one hell of a distraction, the two men were looking for a woman.

And it wasn't the mystery blonde." He turned in his chair so all of him was facing all of her. "I think they wanted you, and, considering how they met us with bats and gunfire, I'm pretty sure you don't want them to find you."

NIGHT CAME TO find them all exhausted. Mel chief among them, even though she wouldn't admit it.

"I'm fine," she said, unprompted, one more time.

Sterling wasn't convinced.

Even more so when they pulled up to her old house and went through the process of grabbing her things.

When they were back in his truck, she let out a breath so deep that every part of her shrank.

He hated seeing it.

"I can stay at the hotel," she said after he started the truck again. "Is it even still open? I could—"

"You can stay at my place," Sterling interrupted.

Mel turned to give him a look that he knew to be stuck between stubbornness and defiance. He shook his head at it.

"If we're right and all of these roads lead back to you, there's no way I'm letting you out of my sight until we have more answers," he said. "If you'd rather we go to a hotel or motel or just spend the night in the truck, that's fine by me. Personally, I'd rather go somewhere I know has a fridge filled with leftovers and that also happens to have great water pressure for a much-needed shower."

Mel's blue eyes searched him for a moment.

Then he knew she'd given in.

"Okay."

Sterling was glad to leave Rider Partridge's mansion and head off across Kelby Creek into the darkness if it meant he was finally going home. Though, when he turned on the street that led up to the house, Mel didn't seem to feel the same.

"Wait."

She sat straighter in her seat as Sterling pulled into the driveway.

"Listen, I have a guest bedroom, and even though it's small it'll work just fine," he defended. "I won't even bother you once we get in. Just give you a quick tour and you can have the run of the house."

Mel shook her head.

"No. That's not what I meant." She went back to looking at the house. The garage light was on, and he could see the light over the sink in the kitchen he always left on. "I— This is where you live."

It wasn't a question, but she was surprised.

"Yeah. For a few months now."

Something was still stumping her.

"You moved. I mean, from the house on Tally Street. I—I didn't know that."

Sterling felt the constant motion of the last day and a half finally slow. Then the weight of the time spent away from each other settle.

Not only had Mel left him in the dust, she hadn't even bothered to look back to see how it had settled.

"Yeah. I moved five years ago."

He could see it in her face despite the low light.

She'd really had no idea.

Sterling tried to keep his emotions in check, but he heard the hardness in his voice when he added on one last bit before getting out of the truck.

"You weren't the only one who left Kelby Creek behind. The only difference is, I chose to come back."

Chapter Nine

The shower was great.

Still, Mel felt like sobbing into the hot water. The only reason she didn't had to do with the man walking around the kitchen, cooking for them.

For her.

Despite everything.

Despite her leaving.

Mel felt guilt unlike any other pulse around her heart. In all this time, she'd never checked up on Sterling—she hadn't wanted to risk it. She'd just pictured him doing what he always had.

Waking up in his bedroom on Tally Street, making coffee in his flannel pajama pants by a sink with a chip in it, getting ready and heading out to the department for another day on the job. Then, maybe after, going to the gym or a bar or his father's or Sam's house.

Just living his life. Happy and healthy and in no way altered by her.

Mel let the hot water beat against her back.

He'd moved. Sterling had left Kelby Creek, and she hadn't known.

And when *he* had realized that?

Mel couldn't shake the way his face had shut down.

There wasn't a whole lot in the world Mel felt she was good at, but of the few, hurting Sterling Costner was up there in the top five.

Mel finished the shower while trying to keep her thoughts on neutral ground. She wrapped her hair up in a wet, messy bun. Her tired legs slid through the only sleep shorts she'd brought and she settled into an old high school T-shirt that, miraculously, still fit.

The house smelled like bacon, and Mel followed the scent all the way to the kitchen. A man stood in front of the stove.

But it wasn't Sterling.

Adrenaline shot through Mel's body with such ferocity that she froze in place.

Then, within the next breath, the details started to filter in.

Not as tall as Sterling, but with the same dark hair. A smaller frame and slimmer build, with more freckles across his skin and a small scar on his forearm where he'd crashed his bike one day when they were riding across the bridge out near the creek.

The man turned, spatula in hand, and Mel saw the face of the only other man she'd loved in Kelby Creek smiling at her.

"Sam!"

Mel melted as Sam Costner closed the space between them and wrapped her in a hug. All the guilt of her leaving and cutting off all contact with everyone hit her like a brick again. That brick was added to the one she'd already had thrown at her because of Sterling and was topped by the trauma of the last two days.

It was too much for Mel.

So she cried into Sam's shoulder like she had the day Rod Johnson stood her up for prom and the day she'd found out her mother was moving away.

Sam let her, because Sam had always been one of the best people she knew.

And Sterling understood all that.

Mel could hear him moving around the kitchen behind them. When she finally pulled away, wiping at her face, she saw three plates of breakfast food on the table.

"Sam, want a beer?" Sterling asked, as if everything was normal.

Sam was game.

"Only if it's the good kind. Last time you tried to cheat me with the cheap stuff."

He smiled down at Mel and gave her a little nod.

She returned it, sniffling.

"Mel?" Sterling turned to her. Eyes as blue as they had been the first day they'd met. He didn't smile, but he wasn't looking at her like she'd just broken him. "The *good* beer, OJ or some water?"

Mel's smile grew. It was genuine.

"Who am I to turn down some good beer?"

THE FOOD WAS GOOD. The company was better.

Mel finally took it easy on herself and let the guilt and shame take a break while she enjoyed being with the Costner boys. Even though the years had stretched between them, Sam was still more or less the same.

Though he did look more tired than usual. Something he explained by way of pulling out his phone to show her a picture.

"And *this* is my daughter, Linney."

Mel scooped up the phone and absolutely cooed at the adorable red-haired baby covered in freckles on the screen.

"You have a *daughter*?" she repeated with a squeal attached. "Oh, Sam! She's so precious!"

Sam laughed.

"If you ask Robbie his feelings on her now that she's going through sleep regression, he'll tell you she's preciously the worst."

Mel scoffed.

"One thing I remember clearly about Robbie was his undying desire to have a bunch of kids. I'm sure he does almost nothing but dote on her. You, too."

Sterling pointed his beer bottle at her.

"You got that right. Don't let Sam *or* Robbie fool you. That is exactly how they both are," he said. "Doting and overprotective. Dad's been trying to take Linney for one night a week to give them a break, and the best he's been able to do was convince them to let him come over and watch her every Wednesday. Even then I'm pretty sure they watch him on the baby monitor."

Mel felt her heart squeeze at that. Callahan Costner was a good, wholesome man who loved his family completely. He'd never once wavered in understanding, support and compassion for them or for the people they cared about. Which, at one point, had included her.

Sam shrugged.

"Okay, listen. Linney might be a poop monster sometimes, but she's our poop monster, and that means a whole lot. Complaining and loving all mixed together."

They all laughed.

Mel wished they could stay in this feel-good bubble all night. She knew they couldn't. The conversation finally took a turn for the dark. She was glad she at least had a good beer for it.

Sam looked at his brother.

"Speaking of Dad, he heard about Rose through the grapevine, which I think is probably the main reason he called."

"Let me guess—he wouldn't say who was at the head of that grapevine?"

Sam shook his head.

"Mr. Kessler isn't one to gossip much, but he's a part of the rotary club, and they gab more than most if given the right piece of news. Rose Simon was the talk of the town back in the day, and her being back and being killed… Well, not many are going to pass up talking about that."

"What exactly did he tell Dad?"

Sterling's brow lined with tension. Mel's stomach tightened.

"Just that he'd heard she was killed…at Rider Partridge's old house." Sterling took a quick pull of his beer. Sam shifted his gaze to Mel. "From what I was able to gather, no one knows you were in the house, though."

Mel wasn't surprised that Sam was already caught up on what had really happened. Once again, the Costner boys had always been close. She *was* surprised that it hadn't leaked out that Mel had been on scene with Rose's body. The sheriff's department had become a lot better at keeping things under wraps since the last time she'd been in Kelby Creek.

"But people do know I'm in town," Mel said. "Jonathan let me know that much when he came to see me in the hospital."

Mel could tell Sam didn't want to nod, but he did.

"Your name was already popping up before the news about Rose broke."

Sterling set his bottle down a little too hard on the table. It made both of their heads snap to attention. He didn't apologize.

"Rose wasn't killed at that house," he almost growled. "She was moved after the fact. If people stopped long enough to get their facts straight, this whole town would be better off. And don't get me started on Jonathan Partridge. He had no right to show up at the hospital and try to intimidate you to leave town. If anyone should be intimidated to leave anyplace, it's him."

Sam agreed with a hearty nod.

Mel opened her mouth to third the notion when a thought popped into her head and she paused.

Sterling's brow scrunched at the sight.

"What is it?"

"The house," Mel said simply.

"What about it?" asked Sam.

Mel's heartbeat started to speed up a little. She put her napkin down and went to the guest bedroom to get her phone off the charger. She hurried back. Sterling had his chair pushed out, waiting.

"It has a security system where you can't open any of the doors or main-floor windows without tripping the alarm. Once you do that, you have thirty seconds to put in a code before the sirens start going off and the police get dispatched."

"You disarmed it when I dropped you off after the hospital on Monday night," Sterling added.

Mel nodded.

"And now we know that poor Rose was already in the bedroom. Which means—"

She opened the security company's app on her phone and logged in. Sterling was already on the same wavelength.

"Which means someone had to turn it off *and* set it before then."

Mel searched for the records of use.

Sam wasn't convinced.

"Isn't this something you already told the detectives about? Surely they would have asked to see who had access," he said.

Mel nodded.

"This is what I showed Detective Lovett." Mel found what she was looking for and turned the phone around to show the men. Both leaned forward, brows drawn together in attention. "These are the time stamps for when the keypad was accessed and the alarm was turned off and on again. The top line is me turning off the system to let everyone in after I found Rose, the one before that was me turning it on after you dropped me off and the one before that was me turning it off right when we showed up." Mel ran her finger down to the next time stamp. "This was a week ago when the cleaning crew came in and turned it off and on again. Which is what I told Detective Lovett. Now, see, the security system is hardwired. It doesn't have a battery backup. It was an extra feature I decided not to pay for since, honestly, I was hoping the house would just kind of be forgotten by everyone."

Mel turned her phone back around and went to a different app.

"Which means the only thing that can turn the security system off without tripping the alarm is when the power goes off. Instead I get an email alert letting me know when the power went off and when it came back on. Neither gets logged."

She found what she was looking for, buried beneath several other emails. It was unopened.

Mel clicked it and turned the phone back around.

"The system went off-line Monday at 1:23 p.m."

"And according to this didn't come back on until 2:32 p.m.," Sam read.

Mel looked at Sterling. This time he pulled out his phone.

"Your security system was off for more than an hour," he said.

"And considering there were no storms in the area and I was in the hospital—"

"There's a good chance the killer cut your power, probably flipped your breaker, to move Rose's body inside," Sam finished.

Mel handed her phone over while Sterling scrolled through his, looking for a number.

"Does this help?" she asked.

Sterling stood up. Mel could already hear the phone ringing as the call went through.

He nodded, expression severe.

"Rose's estimated time of death was around one thirty. If she was killed outside the house, then that means she probably wasn't killed that far from it. You may have just narrowed down the search for where she was murdered by more than half."

SAM LEFT AROUND TEN. Mel said good night right after. Sterling was in his own bed by eleven.

When midnight rolled around, he was back on his feet and trudging through the hallway to the kitchen for some water. He wasn't exactly thirsty, but it was something to do to occupy his mind other than just lying in bed, staring up at the ceiling.

Apparently, he wasn't the only one with the same plan.

The kitchen light over the sink was on. Mel stood beneath it. There was a glass of water in her hands and a faraway look on her face as she stared out the window.

For a moment, Sterling thought about not disturbing her.

She looked too peaceful.

A far cry from earlier when she'd finally broken down on his brother's shoulder.

Sterling knew then that he should have brought Sam into the fold earlier. Seeing the two best friends reconnect without a word exchanged between them had been a silent reminder that Sterling hadn't been the only one to lose her.

Mel jumped. She must have seen him out of the corner of her eye.

Her hand went to her chest in surprise.

Sterling walked the rest of the way in.

"Sorry," he said. "I was debating whether or not to disturb you. I came in here for a drink."

Mel patted her chest and shook her head.

"No, it's fine. I *am* in your house just gazing out your windows when I should be sleeping." She lifted her own glass. "I also needed an excuse to stop tossing and turning in bed."

Sterling gave her a genuine laugh.

"Great, troubled minds."

He reached over her for a glass and went to the refrigerator for some water. When he was done, Mel had found a new spot leaning against the oven door. Sterling mirrored her stance and leaned against the counter opposite her.

For another long moment, Sterling wanted to just look at her. To wonder about her without that true-blue gaze searching him.

Without the weight of questions pressing against both of them.

But it was Mel who dived headfirst into several conversations he was ready to avoid until the morning.

"Has Detective Lovett gotten back to you yet?"

Sterling shook his head.

"No, but he said the information would definitely help. He also said he'd keep me updated."

Mel sighed again.

And then continued.

"You know, despite the circumstances, it was nice to see Sam." A small smile pulled up the corner of her lips. "Thank you for calling him in."

Sterling took a sip of water and shrugged.

"Who said it was for you two? Maybe I just wanted someone to come over and complain about some of my beer."

That smile grew.

"Either way, it was nice. So was the beer."

Sterling did a little bow.

"I try."

Mel took a long pull of her water. She didn't look away when she was done. Instead her smile fell. She held his stare with a viselike intensity.

"I went to Huntsville."

She let her words linger for a second. Then followed them up quickly.

"After I left, I went and stayed in a hotel in Huntsville for a week," she continued. "Then I got a job as a barista at a coffee shop. I worked there for six months until a reporter found me. He was trying to make a name for himself and wouldn't leave me alone. It brought everything back up, so I left. A coworker felt bad for me and got me a job at a coffee place with her friend in Birmingham. I lived with a woman named Deirdre and her son for a little bit, then another barista for a bit more, and then met my current boss one day at work.

"I was manager of the coffee shop for a while and wrote articles for my current boss on the side until she offered me a full-time spot as a writer and technical designer. I got my own apartment in a nice neighborhood two years ago and have lived alone since. It's a small one-bedroom, but I can walk to the store if I want, and I also have a spot in the parking garage for my car, which is nice."

Mel hesitated briefly but her words stayed strong. "I dated one man I met at the coffee shop for five months before I broke it off, have been on three other separate dates that ended in disaster and thought about touring Europe alone until I realized just how much money I didn't have. Dad still doesn't talk to me, but Mom has been calling me on my birthday and Christmas, which is progress for her. I got a tattoo on my right hip last year and finally watched *Game of Thrones* and have been thinking about adopting a dog."

Mel put her glass down on the counter behind her and took a step forward. There was still a foot between them. Sterling didn't move.

"And I realized tonight that I have no right in the world to ask you about your life without at least offering up what I've been doing with mine, so that's why I just rambled to you. Because I *do* want to know about yours."

Mel snapped her mouth shut. True to her word, she'd said her piece.

Now she was looking at Sterling, waiting to see if he'd say his.

But in the low light of his kitchen, staring at a woman he would have been married to for five years now had he had his way, he couldn't bring himself to tell her the truth about his time spent away from Kelby Creek.

She must have seen it in his expression.

Mel did a little nod.

"That's okay," she said. "You don't owe me anything. Honestly. I'll just see you in the morning, okay? Good night."

Mel moved faster than a blink. She left Sterling standing there feeling every way a man could feel.

It wasn't until he heard her bedroom door shut that he poured his water out with a low curse.

He went to bed right after.

Chapter Ten

The town's sirens woke Sterling up.

But if they hadn't, his phone blaring would have.

Their tornado watch had turned into a tornado warning.

Sterling was out of bed in an instant. He swiped his phone, unlocked it with his thumb and was at the guest bedroom door all in one quick movement. There wasn't time for niceties or privacy. Sterling opened the door already calling Mel's name.

She might have been gone from their neck of the woods for five years but Mel had grown up in South Alabama. She knew the drill, too. Her hair was framing a face fresh from sleep, but she was standing at the door, her own phone in hand. The only difference was she'd been quicker on the draw and had her Facebook app open. Sterling recognized their local weatherman, Todd Decker, at the helm. He was talking fast, but Sterling listened to Mel.

"He said it was spotted near Wynn Road heading west. Isn't that near here?"

Sterling didn't waste time. He slipped his hand around Mel's and pulled her along to the hall closet. It was small and lined with flimsy wooden shelves filled with towels, sheets and extra blankets.

Sterling grabbed the shelves as quickly as he could and pulled them out. Mel stood back while he made up the room just as the power cut out. Her phone stayed on, the only source of light. Todd Decker had his voice raised and was pointing to the map. Sterling didn't hear the specifics, but "Seek shelter immediately" was enough.

He kicked the discarded shelves and linens aside and pushed Mel into the slightly bigger space. Sterling had every intention of staying outside the door, but Mel hooked his arm.

"Come on!"

The wind outside was hellish against the house. Sterling folded around Mel to make the small space work and shut the door. Todd Decker's voice fell somewhere to the ground.

"Where's Wynn Road?" Mel asked against his chest.

Sterling hated to tell her the truth.

"We're on Wynn."

It was like the tornado was waiting for him to drop the punchline. No sooner than the words were out of his mouth did the world around them get loud. Todd became a murmur in the dark. All Sterling could do was put his head over Mel's and became a cage around her. Mel only strengthened the hold by pressing into him, arms circling his waist.

All they could do after that was wait.

And wait.

And wait..

HE MADE IT to the house in time to watch the weather report on the tornado tearing through Kelby Creek. He wasn't the only one who was plugged into the news.

"It's saying it dragged from John Riley Drive, past Wynn Road, before popping up around Hartley," his companion reported. "Wynn is where that Costner guy is, isn't it?"

He balled his fists. He was seeing red.

"Yeah. That's where *that Costner guy* is. But, more importantly, that's where Melanie is."

The other man rubbed his chin and shook his head. He was still looking at the live report streaming from his phone.

"They're saying there's a few houses that got damaged and a lot of trees down, but no one can say if anyone's dead yet."

"That would be just fine luck. After all of this time, after all of this effort, and Melanie would up and get killed by a tornado of all things."

He swore deep, low and with a ferocity that caught the other man's attention. He lowered his phone and tried to look hopeful.

"We can still do this if she's gone. We don't *need* her. If anything, this might be a blessing in disguise, you know? The last two times we've tried to grab her, she's managed to get away. I mean, because of her and her friend, Luis is probably brain-dead in the hospital." He tried to motion to himself. It made him look even more pathetic lying there hooked up to an IV on the makeshift bed. "Look at me. If you didn't have your doc connection, I'd be just as bad or worse off. Maybe this is God's way of giving you one."

He didn't mean to lose his temper, but one moment he was on the other side of the room at his desk and in the next he had his finger pressed on the man's bandage at his shoulder.

The man roared in pain but knew not to try and fight back.

"*You* aren't a part of this. *You* are here only because I need you now. *You* don't get to say one way or the other what importance Melanie has to my plan. *You* certainly don't get to say her death would be a blessing." He applied a quick spike of pressure. The other man groaned. "And while we're on the subject of Luis, if I had to pick between you and him, you'd be the one in a coma in the hospital and Luis would be right here, squirming under my finger. Because while he might have dropped the ball, he at least remembered not to disobey my *one* rule. Do you remember what that one rule was?"

The other man was sweating now.

His face was pinched.

Still, he answered.

"Under no circumstance do we kill Melanie Blankenship."

He lowered his face to the paling man.

"*Under no circumstance do we kill Melanie Blankenship,*" he repeated. "And yet, you shot at her. Several times. Is that following the rule?"

"No," the man bit out. "I'm sorry."

"I don't care about your apology, but since I owed your father, I saved your life." He finally lifted his finger and stood tall. "I'm considering that debt paid. If you disobey me or so much as wish death on Melanie again, I'll kill you myself. Understood?"

The other man was quick to nod.

"Good. Now, since you can't go be useful and our favorite lawyer is busy, I suppose I need to be the one to leave this charming hideout." He made sure the buttons of his shirt were in line with his belt buckle and nodded. "I need to see if my ex-wife is dead or not."

MEL OPENED HER eyes against the warmth of Sterling's bare chest. She could feel his heartbeat against her cheek. His arms were wrapped around her and not budging an inch.

And, for a second, she thought it would be nice to stay like that.

Yet the quiet world around them was too loud.

"Is it over?" she asked, her voice as wobbly as her legs. Mel had been through two tornado scares in her life and was lucky enough to walk away unharmed and with no damage. She hoped this was her third time.

Sterling was the first to move.

"I think so."

With one hand he pulled his cell phone from his pocket and turned on the flashlight. That light directed down at her.

"Are you okay?" he asked.

"I think I have more adrenaline in me than when I was dangling in the air after falling through the ceiling at the Meeting House, but, other than that, yeah, I'm okay."

Even though she answered, Sterling brought his hand to the side of her face. His palm was as warm as his chest. It cupped her cheek and tilted her chin up higher so he could look into her eyes. He rubbed his thumb along her cheekbone.

Mel felt several butterflies dislodge at the gesture.

Those butterflies were thrown directly into the storm of fear still raging within her.

Sterling searched her face and nodded.

Then he let her go completely and opened the closet door.

Mel felt an insurmountable amount of relief that the hallway was still there.

Sterling was less enthused.

"If a tree didn't hit this house, I'll give you everything in my bank account."

He shone his phone's flashlight down the hallway toward the front of the house. The power was still off, but the structure looked intact. Mel turned her light on and shone it toward the back half.

There was nothing out of the ordinary there.

Mel walked slowly to the guest bedroom door and peeked inside. There were mud and leaves stuck to the outside of the window but no damage. She turned around and went to Sterling's room.

Mel sucked in a breath.

Sterling was at her side with his light on.

The two windows on either side of his bed were shattered. Giant limbs stuck through where they should have been.

Sterling's light tilted up.

"I had a feeling the maple would fall. At least it didn't come through the roof. It must have caught on the smaller tree that was right next to it." He started to go to the window.

Mel grabbed his hand and squeezed.

"You're barefoot and there's glass everywhere. Hold on."

She let go and hurried to the guest bedroom. She jumped into her tennis shoes and was back in the master bedroom looking for his shoes. Mel found them on the other side of the bed. She paused by the dresser and pulled out a pair of socks and an undershirt and then went to a lower drawer for some jeans. Sterling might have moved, but how he organized his clothes hadn't changed.

"I know you're about to go a mile a minute, and there's no point doing it in your nightclothes," Mel explained, bringing them back and crunching over broken glass in the process. "Go get changed in the hallway so you don't hurt yourself."

Sterling took the clothes with a nod, but his cell phone started ringing.

Mel saw by the caller ID that it was Sam.

She took his phone and shooed him.

"Go put that stuff on. I'll talk to him."

Sterling didn't complain.

"Yes, ma'am."

Sam was talking non-stop as soon as Mel answered the phone.

"We're good," she assured him. "It looks like a tree fell against the house, though. Not enough to cave anything in, but definitely enough to blow his bedroom windows out and damage the siding."

Mel walked across the broken glass again carefully and tried to look out past the branches. It was still raining and way too dark.

"That was the last storm front supposed to come through," Sam said. "But the rain might pick up a little before it's all gone. I'll call Dad and we'll be over in ten. Tell Sterling we'll bring the chain saw, but I think he has the plastic sheeting in the garage that we can use to cover the openings."

Mel's gaze went over to the bed, following a long limb that had twisted and jabbed downward.

Right into the bed.

Her stomach went cold at that.

What if Sterling hadn't gotten up when he had?

"Tell him to bring lanterns." Sterling was behind her. He'd dressed in record time. "I have a flashlight, but I'd rather have something to put down in case the power doesn't come back soon."

Mel opened her mouth to relay the request, but Sam had already heard it.

"Got it," he said. "We'll be over in ten."

Sam ended the call.

"They're bringing the chain saw, but you have the plastic sheeting in your garage." Mel's voice was flat to her ears. She was still looking at the limb. "We're out of danger for another tornado, but Sam said we're still going to get a little rain."

Mel wasn't looking at Sterling, but she felt him stand next to her, as easy as breathing.

She felt a different kind of weight pressing into her

chest. All she could see was the punctured sheets and mattress. Leaving him had been hard. Losing him? That feeling burned itself through her heart with such heat her eyes started to water.

Sterling couldn't see that.

Not in the low light, not with her facing away.

Instead, he was trying to find some humor.

"Sam'll be a grinning fool to hear that him staying on me all these years to keep my phone charging at night finally paid off," he said. "That phone alert was no joke. I didn't even know my phone could be that loud."

Sirens sounded in the distance. First responders.

Sterling's phone started to ring.

"I was wondering when Marigold would reach out. I'm sure Brutus will be next."

He started to turn away, but Mel was faster.

She grabbed his hand to get his attention. When he faced her and she knew she had it, Mel did the only thing that felt right.

She pushed up on the tips of her toes and pressed her lips against his with a world of gratitude.

Sterling didn't get a chance to react before she ended the kiss.

"I sure am glad that you're a light sleeper, Sterling Costner," she said with feeling.

Mel slid her hand down to his chest and patted it twice. She sniffled but didn't linger. Instead she let the man go and headed to the door while glass crunched underneath her shoes.

"I'll go get a broom."

Chapter Eleven

Ms. Martha was out in her housecoat. Marigold was in a dress and with a man wearing a casual suit. The Costner men were dressed in rain jackets, jeans and water boots. Deputy Park and half the department were in uniform.

Everyone was helping with something.

Sterling had been fortunate in the fact that the lone tree to fall in his yard had only damaged the side of his house and not his roof, like Mr. Sinclair across the street—he had a tree splitting his one-story and his neighbor's car that had started in the driveway had ended up in the side yard, upside down and crunched.

There was more damage up the road where the tornado had actually touched down and run long, but, as best as they could tell half an hour into everyone trying to assess the damage, no one had been killed. A few, however, were taken to the hospital for cuts or bruises. Marigold's date said he'd heard that an elderly man two roads over had a broken arm from where a cabinet had fallen on him. Not the best news, but a lot better than it could have been.

Sterling repeated that sentiment when the sheriff arrived.

Brutus clapped hands with Sterling's father, asked quickly about Sam's daughter and had a hand on Sterling's back as he surveyed the tree both were about to start cutting away from the house.

"I hate when they hit at night," Brutus said with a deep sigh. "They already have the audacity to be wild, unpredictable devils, and then they go and do it when no one can see a damn thing."

"Night tornados definitely aren't my favorite," Sterling agreed.

Brutus nodded. The power was still off, but Sam had pulled through with several battery-powered lanterns. He'd never been a fan of the dark, so he always made sure to be prepared for it. Something Sterling was going to have to double down on in the future.

"I heard Melanie's here. She okay, too?"

Sterling was glad the dark probably hid the fact that he tensed.

Not so much because Brutus was talking about Mel, but because he still was partially processing what had happened.

Sleep. Tornado. Mel kissing him.

A man could only handle so much at one time.

"She's good. Was already up and ready when it was time to go into the hall closet. She took over cleaning up the mess in the house. Even was smart enough to start moving some of my things to another room so they wouldn't get ruined."

Brutus nodded again.

"That's good."

He went quiet for a bit. Sterling gave him a long look.

"If you want to say something but are trying to find a way to get it out, I'd prefer the direct approach," Sterling said. "I can tell something's bothering you."

If Brutus had been wearing his cowboy hat, Sterling was sure he would have taken it off and placed it on his chest. Like it was a barrier that could keep him protected from the world around them.

His head was hat-free, though, and he kept his words frank.

"The reason I came by wasn't just to check on you," Brutus started. "I came because Cole found a lead that might just be what we've been waiting for."

Sterling turned so his back was to the house. He was ready.

"What is it?"

Brutus lowered his voice. No one was around them.

"Rose's car was spotted at a gas station the morning of her death. She was in a heated conversation with a man, and they both left in a visible huff. We couldn't hear what they were saying, but it was easy to see the man was Jonathan Partridge." Brutus held up his hand to stop Sterling from reacting prematurely. "Foster is already trying to run him down and, I have to say, it could be nothing, but—"

"But it would a damned coincidence that Jonathan Partridge fought with the late Rose Simon the morning of her murder and on the same day that Mel comes to town and is attacked," Sterling interrupted. He was heated and only getting hotter. "And we all know his feelings for Mel are nothing but hate. Especially after the fire."

Brutus kept his hand up to slow Sterling down.

"I'm not here to say that he isn't involved, or even behind whatever this is," Brutus said. "I'm here to tell you that, until we find Jonathan for some questioning, you sound the red alert if you see him. That goes double for Melanie. Her run-in with him in her hospital room should be the last time she's alone with him until we get this all figured out."

Sterling was huffing now. He nodded.

"What about the gunman in the hospital? Any ID on him yet?"

Brutus shook his head.

"He's in a coma, but nothing is popping on our databases. Foster's been on it, though. I reckon it won't be long."

"I guess they're still looking for where Rose was killed, too, huh?"

This time Brutus nodded.

Sterling made an impolite noise.

The sheriff didn't seem to mind. If anything, he sympathized.

"You know how these things work half the time," he said. "We go from knowing a few things to learning a lot all at once. When it rains, it pours. Pardon the phrase." He nodded to the sky. It had stopped raining, but it definitely had been pouring.

Sterling grit his teeth.

"It's the other half that has me worried," he admitted after a moment.

"The other half?"

Sterling sighed.

"The other times where we only ever know a few things, they never make sense and we're stuck with more questions than answers." He rubbed his jaw, then turned back to face his house at the sheriff's shoulder. "I don't know what's going on, and I can't help if I don't know what's going on."

Brutus clapped him on the back. When he spoke again, his voice had gone from gruff to a slightly softer gruffness.

"When I took this job—the second time—I was so frustrated that I couldn't fix everything wrong and bad about what had happened on my first day. That stress came around at the end of my first week. Followed me to the end of my first month, and near about the end of my first year, my wife sat me down and said something that sounded ridiculous. But boy, I tell you what, it's done wonders for me since."

Sterling faced the older man, genuinely curious.

Brutus's smile was easy to see despite the dark.

"'You can only ever kiss the person right in front of you.'" That smile of his grew into a grin. Sterling felt his eyebrow raise. Brutus laughed. It was genuine. Then he grew serious within the span of a breath. "You can only control so much in this life, Sterling. That goes double for this line of work. Beating yourself up or running yourself ragged to solve everything all at once isn't going to do anyone any good."

"Because you can only kiss the person right in front of you," Sterling repeated.

Brutus tipped his head down as if he was wearing an invisible cowboy hat.

Sterling thought a moment on that.

Then he was smiling, too.

But not because of Mrs. Chamblin's weirdly appropriate piece of advice.

No.

Sterling was looking at his house and thinking about a real kiss.

And a real woman he'd like to share another one with.

Brutus might or might not have picked up on that fact. He cleared his throat and put his thumbs through his belt loops.

"Well, I've got to head on out. I'm glad you're okay, son."

A thud sounded, and the chain sawing stopped. They shook hands, and thoughts of kissing went to the back burner as Sterling hurried to see what his father and Sam had done. He didn't see the sheriff drive away, and he didn't see when Marigold's date drove up with his truck and more tools to help secure the side of Sterling's house. He also didn't see, though he heard, when a few people from up the road came to talk to his father, who was taking a break and talking about the damage everyone had sustained. Sterling also didn't see Mel for a bit, mostly because she said she was focused on moving more of his things so they didn't take on any more water.

And maybe he was using his own focus as an excuse to keep his distance.

Because, as much as he shouldn't, he wanted to press his lips to hers, feel her body against his and forget about the last five years for a while.

So he did the work outside and gave her space inside, and of all the things he didn't see in the darkness, he sure hadn't seen the man across the street.

Watching.

Waiting.

Ready.

THE GLASS CAME up without much fuss. The tree limbs penetrating the bed were a lot trickier. Mel hated looking at the twisting, gnarled things making holes in the mattress through a torn blanket and sheets. She was stuck in a loop of what-if for a man she'd left in the dust.

It was driving her crazy.

When the Costner men finally came in to saw away the branches and tarp up the window, she could have cried with distracted relief, because when they went back outside to deal with the bulk of the tree, it left Mel with a new job.

She stripped Sterling's mattress, inspecting the holes with a quick eye, and put all the linens in a garbage bag. Apart from the gashes, the mattress itself wasn't wet, so she decided to cover the nasty reminders and went to the closet she'd been hiding in hours before. She went through the motions of straightening the closet up, taking out new sheets, and was walking back to the bedroom with her small lantern in one hand and a bundle in the other when something caught the corner of her eye.

In a plastic tub she'd filled with things from the top of Sterling's dresser and nightstand, Mel saw that the wooden box his grandfather had given him had shifted open. Had it been anything else, she wouldn't have put everything down to fix it, but it was his trinket box. A family tradition among the Costner men, a trinket box was handmade by a Costner and given to a Costner. Ray had one from his grandfather, Sam had one from his father and Sterling had said many times he couldn't wait to make one for his son or grandson. It was just something the family did.

They made a box for important things, and they gave that box to someone important to them.

It had always been a lovely notion to Mel, especially since she wasn't close with her parents.

So she bent down and picked the box up to make more room for it.

The lid, already open, slid off.

Mel scrambled to catch it before it hit the floor. She made another noise when she was successful.

Then she looked down at the now-open box.

And froze.

The box itself wasn't large but was big enough to hold a few items. There was a bolo that Sterling's uncle had given him from their trip to Texas when he was a teen, a coin made of foil that Sam had made him for his birthday when he was ten, an old picture of his parents when they'd first started dating, and a ring.

Mel grabbed the lantern and held it down to get a better look.

A thin gold band with a single diamond.

It was beautiful.

She'd also never seen it before.

Mel looked around. She could still hear people working outside.

It wouldn't hurt to hold the ring, would it?

Mel picked it up with slightly shaking hands. She didn't know why. It wasn't like it was hers.

Still, she couldn't deny it was exactly what she would have wanted in a ring. There was a pure beauty to something so simple.

A deep sadness shook within her.

Was there someone in Sterling's life whom he wanted to give it to?

The fact that she didn't know hurt almost as much as if she'd been told there was.

Mel shook her head at herself.

Sadness or not, she did something she shouldn't have.

She put it on.

The fit was perfect.

Her heart fluttered.

When someone cleared their throat behind her, that fluttering turned to heat in her cheeks.

She whirled around, already trying to think of an excuse as to why her nosiness had turned into a ring on her finger.

But it wasn't Sterling behind her.

It wasn't a Costner or a neighbor. It wasn't even a stranger.

No.

It was a nightmare in a suit.

"I gave you a ring once. It was a lot bigger than that." Rider Partridge was grinning. "And we saw how that turned out, now didn't we?"

Chapter Twelve

Mel thought she was dreaming. She had to be, right?

If she was, then Dream Her knew instantly that she was in trouble. There were just no two ways about it.

She was sweating something awful the moment she opened her eyes. The fabric of her blouse was sticking to her skin with a slickness that sent a shiver through her. Her hair wasn't faring any better. It was adhered to her forehead like someone had slapped paste on her. She tried to focus on what was going on and found nothing but the easy details around her.

Light poured through windows without curtains in a room that was as unfamiliar as they came. She was on the hard floor, lying on her back. No one else was in a room except for a woman who was also lying on the floor.

Next to Mel.

With eyes closed.

Mel struggled to get up but found her movements sluggish. Every alarm bell in her mind was blaring. It was the only reason she didn't make a noise. She hadn't been awake long enough to determine if she was in immediate danger. Although it wasn't like she'd just woken from a nice slumber.

Regaining consciousness was more of what fit the bill.

Just like she had in the ambulance after the car accident.

She *had* to be dreaming, right?

Mel racked her brain quickly for her last memory.

Just like after the accident, there wasn't a lot to grab.

Mel looked at the woman.

She wasn't moving, and neither was anyone else in the vicinity. Mel took a moment to check herself. The scab from her head injury in the crash was still closed. She was wearing her own clothes but no shoes. Her head hurt, too, but not in a way that she expected. It felt fuzzy. Weird. Otherwise, physically, she seemed okay.

Mel wasn't about to sit still and wait for answers to come to her so she stood, slowly.

The cabin was not unlike other fishing cabins that she'd visited in the South. You could only live so long in a place called Kelby Creek before you actually fished in the creek. This cabin, unlike one you might find in the mountains that was made of charming logs and wood galore, was more function than flair. She was in the main living space with furniture that looked older than her thirty years and a kitchenette in the corner whose heyday had probably been when it was first built. It was also clearly used. There were beer cans littering the surfaces, crushed and tops popped, and the distinct smell of fish in the air. Probably cleaned and cooked right there in the room when there was a catch.

Two doors ran across the back wall, and one was opened to show a bathroom. The other one was closed.

It had a metal clasp at the top with a padlock attached.

Mel felt another shiver go through her at the sight.

The last door was the one behind her. It led outside. Through the window next to it, Mel saw grass, dirt and a dock that hung over water in the distance.

It had to be the creek, right?

Mel hurried to the window to see if there was a vehicle parked outside when the woman on the floor behind her made a noise. A groan of pain.

She felt like a fool for not checking her sooner.

Then again, who was she?

Friend or foe?

The woman let out another sound and shifted her weight. She moved from being prone on her stomach to turning on her side. The woman opened her eyes. She blinked a lot and groaned some more.

She wasn't a particularly big woman, but she was tall. Lean, too, but she wasn't toned or overly muscled. If she carried strength, it was the surprising kind. Something that came out of nowhere when she needed it. She had a tan but not one that look like she spent all day in the sun, and her brown hair was cut short to her chin. She was wearing a yellow blouse and a pair of jeans that had a few holes worn into them. Mel guessed she was younger, maybe early twenties.

Like her, the other woman didn't seem to fit in the cabin.

She also didn't appear to have a weapon on her. At

least not in her hands, and nothing obvious seemed to be protruding from beneath her clothes.

The only move she made was to cradle her head.

Then her eyes finally locked onto Mel's shoes.

The woman was up in a flash, yelling out in pain as she did so.

Mel jumped back like the noise stung her. Her hands went up in defense.

"Whoa, calm down," she hurried. Her throat was dry, along with her mouth. It tasted stale. How long had she been out? Mel pointed to the floor. "I just woke up right there next to you."

The woman was definitely on the younger side. Her flighty look spoke volumes.

She was terrified.

She was in pain.

But, most of all, she was confused.

"What do you mean, you just woke up beside me?" she squawked. "Where are we? What's going on?"

Mel moved her hands to motion for her to bring her volume down.

"I don't know what's going on, but I'm sure yelling isn't going to get us any answers."

That didn't do a thing for the woman. She shook her head and lurched away from Mel.

"Who are you? Where are we?" she rattled off. "Why is my head killing me?"

"I'm Mel, and I have all the same questions." The woman continued to spiral. Mel put her hands out to steady her but stopped before making contact. It focused the woman. She took a visible deep breath. "What's your name?"

"Ella. Ella Cochlin."

That name rang a very small, very far-off bell, but Mel couldn't figure out why. Not when the feeling of urgency was nearly blinding.

"Okay, Ella, what's the last thing you remember?"

"I—I think I was headed to the post office?"

The answer was as sure as Mel felt about what was going on.

"In Kelby Creek?"

Ella nodded.

Well, at least they were most likely still in town.

"What about you? Do you remember anything?"

Mel took a beat to try and recall her last memory again.

"Sterling. My last memory was being with Sterling."

Ella's eyebrows, perfectly manicured, went high in question.

Mel might have flushed had it been any other situation.

Instead, she funneled everything into one question.

What would he do in this situation?

"Do you have your phone?" Mel didn't have hers. She held out hope that Ella might.

It was a hope that died quickly. Ella whimpered out a no, but Mel was already on the move. She searched the room with adrenaline pouring into her veins. Her hands shook something awful.

"Can you see a phone around here or anything that might help us?"

Ella went to looking on her side of the room until they met in the middle.

No phones. No weapons. Nothing useful.

"I may not remember how we got here, but I'm pretty sure we didn't just walk in like we owned the place. We need to leave."

Mel didn't know what had happened from the time she'd been at the house to regaining consciousness in the cabin, but she thought it was safe to jump to three conclusions.

They'd been drugged.

They'd been kidnapped.

And whoever had done both would be back soon.

There was a fourth thought that crawled into Mel's mind, but she decided it the least important issue compared with the others.

Still, she thought it was a bitterness that hurt.

I really shouldn't have come back to Kelby Creek.

THE DAWN CAME and the sun rose to show a neighborhood of extremely tired residents. And those who had helped them.

Sterling's dad left when everyone came to an agreement that now it was someone else's turn to deal with the damage, namely insurance companies and a tree-cutting business. Something most Kelby Creek residents were used to dealing with during their erratic tornado season.

Sam, however, stuck around.

"I've gotten the same amount of sleep being here as I do at home with Linney," he joked, when Sterling tried to shoo him home. "I might as well make us some coffee and eggs before I go."

Sterling was too tired to argue, so he followed his brother into the house.

It was cold and quiet. Not the scene of a close call only hours before. They went back to his bedroom, careful to step quietly in front of the guest bedroom door, and looked inside. Sam spoke low.

"Mel sure did a good job in here. Apart from the plastic sheet over the window, you wouldn't know a tree had tried to say hello while you slept."

Sterling had to agree. Not only had Mel cleaned the room, she'd made his bed with new sheets and a blanket to cover the tears and holes from the branches on top of putting some of his more valuable things in plastic tubs and boxes and moving them to the hallway to stay dry.

It was nice.

"Want me to wake her?" Sam added, looking at the door behind them.

Sterling shook his head.

"I told her to get some sleep after we sawed the branches out of the room but she said she'd only go when she was done cleaning," he said. "Considering all the work she did, I'm betting she needs the rest."

Sam didn't argue, and soon they were both back in the kitchen eating eggs and drinking coffee. Sterling had a plate covered next to them just in case their movement woke Mel, but she still hadn't shown by the time their coffees were drained. He fought the urge to check on her with every swallow of his food and drink.

"Is it weird having her in the house again?"

Sterling gave his brother a questioning look. Sam pointed to his brow with his fork.

"You've been looking at that plate of food with a Sterling-specific intensity that I've only seen when Mel is around," he explained.

If it had been anyone else, he might have waved off the question and comment. But it was Sam, so he told the truth. One he'd never told anyone else.

"You know when she didn't come back that day, when I found her room empty, I felt that. Every moment after for weeks and months, I couldn't get over that feeling. Her *not* being there." Sterling set down his coffee cup. "Then I left and I worked on getting used to me just being me. I made new friends and did new things and then realized how much I wanted to come home to Kelby Creek."

He glanced at the empty chair next to him. "But even then, even as the years went by, I'd catch myself looking for her when I went into another room. Making extra of her favorite food on accident. Even sleeping on the left side of the bed because she preferred the right. I just… If I'm being honest, I'm not sure I ever let myself really believe she was truly gone in the first place. Just in another room I couldn't see. Sleeping in late or at the store grabbing those awful gluten-free cookies she used to be obsessed with. Here, but not really here."

"Gone, but not really gone," Sam added.

Sterling nodded. He let out a long, long breath.

"So, her being here now? Just feels like she took the long way home, even though I know it shouldn't, because she's not back for good."

Sam nodded this time. Sterling didn't think for a moment that he didn't understand him. He was, after all, Sterling's first and best friend. The brothers knew each other completely.

Which was why Sam didn't question the fact that Sterling was romanticizing Mel leaving him high and dry. Sam had probably already known that Sterling hadn't let go. Not completely.

"You know, I never understood why she left in the first place," Sam said, instead. "I thought that after everything was settled with Rider going to prison that she would finally be able to feel free. Or start to heal. I mean, we even had plans to do a big movie night that weekend, and she'd already picked out a movie."

That was news to Sterling.

"Wait. Y'all made plans for after the court date? I didn't know that."

"Yeah. I thought I'd told you."

"Maybe you did," he admitted. "I wasn't exactly thinking straight then."

Sterling tried to remember. He couldn't.

Still, it bothered him.

"What movie?"

"Notting Hill."

That bothered him more.

"Her favorite feel-good movie," he said.

Sam shrugged.

"I thought that maybe that's why she picked it. To throw me off so I wouldn't suspect she was about to run."

Sterling looked back at the chair, like it could answer for Mel, when his phone started to vibrate against the tabletop.

There was no ID, but it was a local number.

"Pretty early for a call. Are you working today?" Sam asked.

"No, I took it off." Sterling answered. "Hello?"

"Sterling, this is Carlos."

He looked at the number again.

"Where are you calling from?"

Carlos Park was a little out of breath. There was a lot of noise in the background. He wasn't at home, that was for sure.

"I'm at the hospital. You heard what happened here the other day? I know you've been busy."

Sterling nodded even though he couldn't see him.

"Yeah. A small fire broke out, right?"

"Yeah. Small but, well, it made for some confusion in the lab," he said. "And I think that was the point."

Sterling gave his brother a questioning look. It was returned.

"What do you mean?"

Sterling didn't understand why Carlos Park was calling him about a hospital fire from the other day, especially so early in the morning.

Though, just as he thought that, he turned his head to look at the doorway leading to the hall.

Carlos spoke fast.

"Amanda—I mean, Dr. Alvarez—had a few questions about some blood work that was taken and, well, she realized that some samples had been swapped around."

Sterling stood.

"Swapped around? Are you talking about Mel's?"

"They're looking into it right now but, yeah, they realized Mel's from the day of the car accident hadn't been logged right." There was more movement on Carlos's end of the line. When he continued his voice had gone low. He was whispering. "They got all squirrelly after finding it and, well, I overheard them say something I thought you should know. I don't know if it's what caused the accident or not, but Sterling, they don't think the car accident is what had Mel unconscious."

Sterling was already walking to the guest bedroom as Carlos kept on.

"She was drugged. And given everything else that's happened, I think it might be safe to assume that she didn't do it to herself. Someone's gunning for your girl, Sterling. Hard."

Sterling had the phone down at his side; Sam was right behind him. He opened the guest bedroom door without knocking.

He'd been hoping to see a messy head of dark hair.

Instead he saw an empty bed.

Sam ran past him to the closed closet. Sterling already knew she wasn't there.

"She could have run again?" he offered. But there was no conviction in his voice.

Sterling went to her suitcase on the floor. Nothing but the clothes she'd been wearing the last time he saw her were missing.

Just like her.

Sterling felt red-hot.

He pulled the phone back to his ear and growled.

"We need to find Jonathan Partridge *now*. Mel's gone and—"

A beep cut through the call. Sterling stopped himself to see another number calling. It was also local.

Hope sprang eternal. Maybe Mel *had* left on her own and was calling to say so?

"Hold on," he told Carlos. He switched over. "Costner here."

The phone call cracked.

So did the voice.

It was Mel.

And she was yelling.

"Sterling! Help us!"

Chapter Thirteen

"Mel?"

Sam motioned wildly through the air, letting his big brother know he had no idea what was going on.

Sterling didn't explain since he had no idea himself.

Mel had yelled for help, then the line had gone silent.

The call had dropped altogether after that.

"Let me call you back," Sterling barked to Carlos as the Call Waiting shifted back to him.

He didn't wait for Carlos to respond.

Sterling stared at the phone for a moment, waiting. Nothing happened.

"Was that her?" Sam's face was drawn with concern. He was no law enforcement officer, but he'd never turned down helping someone when they needed it. Largely in part, no doubt, to how their father had raised them.

"Yeah. She said they needed help."

"They?"

Sterling's phone started to ring again.

"Mel?" he answered. "Where are you?"

This time her voice was low and strained. Whispering with force.

She didn't want to be heard but needed *him* to hear her.

"We're somewhere along the creek. Me and a woman named Ella Cochlin. I think we were drugged, Sterling. Kidnapped. My head hurts and I can't remember how I got here. We woke up in a fisherman's cabin with a dock. We—we followed the creek and found another place maybe a mile up. I—I've never been here before. I broke the window to get in. I'm on the landline."

Sterling wasn't the best at the details. Sure, it would have been a nice skill to claim and it would have made his life easier, but that just wasn't him. Finding Waldo in a crowd took him double the time of others. Yet he didn't stop until he found him. For every detail he missed, he made up for in dedication to get the next.

That said, not one syllable went unheard from Mel's rushed explanation.

Two women, drugged and kidnapped, a fisherman's cabin with dock access, a mile walk along the stream, a structure with a landline but with no occupants.

Sterling took in those details and made sure to lock his emotions out.

Feeding into his rage and concern wasn't going to help Mel now.

Only keeping her safe until he got to her would.

"Okay, Mel, I need you to listen to me." Sterling was walking back through his house. When he got to his car keys, he threw them to Sam. "Are you and Ella alone right now? Why are you whispering?"

They made it outside. Sam understood his assignment. He ran around to the driver's side door.

Sterling was in the truck in a second flat.

"We haven't seen anyone since we woke up. But—but I think there's someone outside."

It tore at Sterling how Mel's voice wavered.

He pushed past it.

"Where are you now? In the house."

He made a phone motion with his hand, and Sam passed his cell phone over.

Sterling might not have been a whiz at the details, but he was good at multitasking. He dialed in a number and hit Call. He passed the ringing phone back over.

"Ask Sheriff Chamblin where he is and tell him we're coming to get him," he said, moving the phone aside to do so.

Sam took to the directions without fussing as Mel's soft voice answered.

"We just hid in the closet. I dropped the phone. That's why I hung up earlier."

"Well, that's good. You two need to keep quiet, but can you tell me anything about the house you're in first?" Kelby Creek was a small town, but in the past ten years or so, a lot of cabins and houses had been built along the creek. They could be anywhere along the length of the town, and that was assuming they were even still *in* town. The creek didn't stop at the town limits. "How big? What color? Any identifying markers outside?"

"Yeah—uh—it's like an ugly gray? Two bedrooms, I think, but small. No garage or carport. No dock, but the water is close and—"

Mel stopped midsentence.

Sterling pulled the phone away from his face to see if the call dropped.

It hadn't.

"Mel?"

When the woman responded, it was barely a whisper.

"Hurry."

The phone went dead again.

Sterling waited to see if Mel would call back.

She didn't.

SHERIFF CHAMBLIN LIVED near the creek himself and was an expert on the area. After retiring from the department, and before he'd come back to help keep it afloat after The Flood, he'd spent many a day fishing along the water. Even after he was back at work, he'd make time to walk along the creek bed with his fishing pole or take out a small pontoon boat to the parts of the creek deep enough to navigate. He knew the area more than most locals.

It was why when Sam sped them to his house, Brutus was already at the curb with a hand-drawn map under his arm and his gun in his holster. He was ready and willing. Though, the gleam of the sheriff's badge in the headlights that caught Sterling's eye reminded him that there was one person inside the truck who didn't have a badge.

"You stay here and call Robbie or Dad to get you. The sheriff won't mind you waiting in the house," Sterling ordered his brother.

Sam shook his head.

"No way. I can drive while y'all talk all of this out."

"Sam, we have no idea what we're getting ourselves into. You don't have a gun or badge."

He shook his head again and smiled.

"I'm not moving, but I *will* stay in the truck at all times. All the heroics left to you two. Promise." Sterling doubled down on his stern look, but Sam wasn't budging. It helped that his reasoning was concrete. "It's Mel, Sterling. We have to help her."

Sterling nodded at that.

Brutus was less concerned with Sam's presence. When Sterling hopped out of the passenger's seat and threw open the back door, they both slid into the back seat without preamble. Sam kept the truck idling as Sterling dived right in with what he knew. He also addressed the fact that they couldn't easily trace the number since Mel had called him directly and not a dispatcher.

"Also…as you can see, Google isn't helping us narrow it down, either," he added, searching the number in his phone's browser as he spoke. "Sometimes we get lucky with that. Not now."

"That's okay. We know enough to start our own search. Like we know that wherever they are, there's power." Brutus was eyeing the map that he'd smoothed out across the middle seat between them. "Which means it could be a rental or occupied by someone who just isn't home right now. Also, not many people have landlines in more modern builds, so let's take a leap and eliminate any newer structures."

He made Xs over a handful of squares representing houses on the map.

"Mel also said they came to in a fisherman's cabin," Sterling said. "One that was a mile or so off following the creek."

"But where they are now doesn't have a dock…"

Sterling was beyond anxious. He tapped his foot and squeezed his phone. Watching Brutus work through his own thoughts was infuriating. Yet, it also made Sterling proud.

Brutus Chamblin might have seen himself as an interim sheriff, but everyone who knew him saw him for what he really was—a great lawman who loved to fish.

He made a few more Xs, leaving twelve or so boxes still on the map without one.

"Tell me word for word what Mel said."

Sterling did so, careful to not forget anything.

Something that worked out for them.

"An ugly gray?" Chamblin repeated.

Sterling nodded, his adrenaline spiking as the sheriff made circles around two of the boxes on the map.

"There are two places that could fit that description. Two that happen to have a fisherman's cabin between them."

"And which one does your gut say they're at?"

Brutus stared at the map. He rubbed at his jaw.

"My wife went out with me one day to fish and commented on how gray doesn't look good on every house…" He tapped the box on the right from him. "This one. I think they're at the Cooper place—a new rental but older build."

Sam was already driving.

"I actually know where that is," he called back.

Brutus pulled his phone out.

"Good, because we're about to make a lot of calls."

Sterling's adrenaline surged again.

"Time to call in the troops?"

Brutus nodded.

"You bet your ass it is."

HER JEANS WERE wet around the ankles, and the cordless phone in her hand was dead.

"The power is out," Mel whispered.

She couldn't see Ella in the darkness of the closet, but she was sure as the sun was hot that the younger woman's eyes were wide with fear. Ella had barely kept it together when they'd come up to the gray house. She'd cried as Mel had used a rock to smash open a back window, and it had only been after they'd heard the splash of what sounded like someone in the water outside that Ella had managed to reel in the louder tears.

Not that Mel was sitting there in the closet judging her.

She was terrified, too.

Even more so now that the power had, she guessed, been cut.

"What—what do we do now?" Ella's voice reminded Mel of a wrung-out towel. She wasn't crying now, but her words were hoarse.

"We stay here and keep quiet. Sterling will come for us."

"But how?" Ella shifted. The closet they'd rushed into barely fit the two of them. Mel could feel the woman's breath against her at the question. "Can they trace the landline? Is that even a thing?"

Mel didn't know. If she had called 9-1-1 and not Sterling's cell phone, maybe they could trace it faster? Or maybe all they needed was a phone number? She wasn't sure how all that worked.

"He'll find us," she said, still flushed with reassurance that Sterling would come. "He'll find us."

If Ella needed more answers than that, she kept her questions to herself.

A minute or two went by with no other sounds than their breathing. The adrenaline that had encouraged them to run from the cabin to the house they were in was long gone from Mel's system. Now she felt exhausted.

Exhausted and more than confused.

It didn't make sense what was happening.

Why had she been taken? And by whom?

And why was Ella there and the kidnapper not?

Mel should have kept her thoughts more positive. Thinking of their kidnapper must have manifested whoever it was. The alarmingly loud sound of a door opening and glass crunching reached into the closet and turned her blood to ice. Ella's hand made it to Mel's arm and turned into a vise.

"Sterling?" Ella's voice was a new level of low whisper.

But Mel wasn't about to answer her.

She listened so hard that it felt like it hurt.

Heavy footfalls walked along the tile of the kitchen, not far from where they were. If it had been Sterling, wouldn't he have announced himself? Wouldn't he have called for her?

Ella's grip tightened exponentially as those footfalls redirected. If there had been any other noise in the house, like the air conditioner, the steps wouldn't have sounded so crisp. So undeniably there.

But they did.

Mel's muscles started to strain in anticipation. She held the cordless phone, envisioning it as a brick instead of hard plastic.

Was it the same people from the Meeting House?

The footsteps thundered into the room next to them and made quick work of righting that wrong before coming into their bedroom.

Mel hunkered down on a scream as those steps settled...

Right outside the closet door.

The pain from Ella's grip became secondary to the fear of what would happen next.

Mel almost closed her eyes to help feel an ounce of protection from it.

Yet, just as her lids started to drop, another sound filled her terrifying world.

Dirt and loose gravel dispersing. Tires rocking to a stop, brakes engaging.

More than one car door shutting.

Whoever was on the other side of the closet door must have gotten a dose of their own medicine. The footsteps retreated at a fast enough speed that Mel couldn't follow exactly where they went in the house.

She did, however, lock onto a new set of sounds entering through what must have been the front door.

"Dawn County Sheriff's Department!"

He didn't need to say her name for Mel to know exactly who had arrived.

"Sterling!"

Mel yelled so loudly for the man that Ella jumped next to her.

She didn't care.

When the new set of footsteps rushed to their hiding place, Mel was already breathing out sweet relief.

Seeing Sterling standing on the other side of the opened door with his gun in one hand, his badge on his belt and his eyes on her was only the icing on the cake.

Chapter Fourteen

Sterling moved his service weapon just in time for Mel's arms to wrap around him. There was nothing but fear in him, and then all he felt was an embrace that was wired with tension.

And obvious relief.

Mel let out a breath against him that Sterling felt all the way through his bones.

She let go and stepped back before he could react. Concern scrunched her brow and widened her eyes.

"Someone was in the room with us when you pulled up," she hurried. "They ran out, but I couldn't tell where they went."

Sterling didn't like that.

He also wasn't about to leave Mel and Ella to go look. He needed them safe first.

"Sam's outside with the truck, and the sheriff is around back. Let's go."

Neither woman bucked at the idea. Ella stood and clutched at Mel's hand within a breath while Mel positioned herself behind Sterling. He almost imagined he could feel her hands on his lower back. He pulled his gun up and focused on navigating the exact way they'd come in, hyperfocused on anyone who wasn't the sheriff or his brother. The house was small but had enough corners to watch out for, and he wasn't keen on doing anything close quarters with two civilians with him. Plus, fighting at the Meeting House had been messy.

He didn't want a repeat.

It felt like a slow walk, but later he'd guess it took less than a minute. They weren't even off the porch before Sam was locking eyes with him. He was out of the truck fast, a liar to his word. Sterling wasn't complaining.

Brutus was nowhere to be found.

Sterling stopped and moved Mel, and with her Ella, around him. He spoke to Sam.

"Get in the truck and get them to the hospital."

"We're not going without you," Mel said at the same time Sam said, "I'm not leaving you."

"We'll be fine. The closest cruiser is less than two minutes out and we don't know—"

The sound of a man yelling made everyone turn.

Brutus.

"Sam. Truck. Now."

Sterling heard a truck door open as he turned around and hustled to the side of the house. Mel hadn't exaggerated—the water was close. So close that when Sterling rounded the last corner he saw Brutus stumble from the grass into the creek.

"Sheriff!"

Sterling swept the area with his gun while running over. There was no one around and no obvious sign of injury on the older man. Except for the pained expression on his face and the fact that he was on his side in the shallow water.

"Sheriff?" Sterling repeated, lowering his gun but not holstering it yet. "What's wrong? Who did this?"

Brutus's eyes were almost closed.

Sterling used his free hand to pull the man up to keep his face from the creek.

Brutus made a noise at the effort.

He was hurting.

A lot.

"Sheriff?"

This time the older man answered.

"My—my heart."

Then his body went limp.

STERLING WAS A sagging mess of worry and wilted anger when he came into Mel's hospital room later that day. Had she not been her own sagging mess in a hospital bed, she would have embraced him.

"They say if Brutus had been alone and had the heart attack, they don't think he would have made it." He dropped into the chair next to the bed. The doctor had just left, but she wasn't about to tell him that. Not when his mind and heart were being dragged around at the same time. "Since we already had everyone on standby, the ambulance made it there even faster than it would have normally. The timing of it all probably saved his life. The doc said Brutus was lucky, all things considered. Now we just wait to see if he keeps that streak up."

"Oh, Sterling."

Mel reached out, but it didn't do much good. Once Sam had gotten her and Ella to the hospital in a blaze of speeding glory, she'd gone from feeling afraid and tired to sick and tired. Her first hour of the stay had been a blur. The dizziness had only stopped a few hours beforehand but, still, she wasn't keen on moving around too much. After Sterling had come in with the ambulance and the sheriff, he'd only left her side long enough to talk to a colleague or doctor. When he wasn't in the chair next to her, Detective Lovett or Sam had been. That was to speak nothing of the uniforms in the hallway, guarding her and Ella's doors. They were still going over what happened to Ella. If they'd gotten a better understanding of it, they hadn't updated Mel yet.

Sterling scraped his chair across the tile until his knees were butted up to the side of the bed. Taking one of her hands in his was easy after that. Mel marveled at how small her hand was within his. Also how warm he was.

She tried to give him a smile that had some warmth, too.

"He's tough. He'll make it."

Sterling nodded, but there was some hesitancy there.

"I talked to his wife just now, too. Turns out she's been worried about his stress levels since he came back to the department." His sigh dragged his shoulders even farther down. "The man was trying to kiss too many people after all."

Mel's eyebrow went sky-high at that, but a knock on the door marked the second appearance of the day from Detective Lovett.

This time his notebook was gone, and he had a friend.

Cole Reiner waited for Detective Lovett to take a seat. He stood off to the side of it.

Sterling let go of her hand.

Both men saw the movement, but neither commented on it.

"So, I know the doctor already went over everything with you two about the drugs in your system, but, since my wife and I had a personal experience with it a few years back, I thought I'd give you the less technical side." Detective Lovett sounded tired. Still, Mel was enraptured by every word.

"The street name for them is Sleepers. Not the most inventive thing, but it's mostly accurate. They're like sleeping pills mixed with Xanax with some steroids thrown in. With a controlled amount, they can make you lose consciousness fast and stay that way for a fair amount of time. My wife and I were dosed with a very small amount and were unconscious for several hours. We also lost some memory right before we lost consciousness. About half an hour, we guessed."

"Which is what happened to me the second time around," Mel said. "The last thing I remember was sweeping up glass while everyone was outside. Then nothing until the cabin."

Sterling tensed. It caught both men's eyes, but Detective Lovett continued.

"You didn't have a lot in your system, the same with Ms. Cochlin. Just enough to knock you out and keep you from remembering who did it. Which, I might add, is why Sleepers *are* popular with some people. Even though they have a higher, and somewhat unpredictable, fatality rate."

It was Mel's turn to tense.

"And that's why the doctor said I was lucky. When I came into town, I apparently had triple the amount I had in me today. That's why I lost so much time."

Mel fought the urge to touch her neck. There was an injection site the doctor had found there that had bruised. Near it was a small scab from another. They hadn't seen it the first time since everyone had thought she'd simply been in a car accident.

Detective Reiner crossed his arms over his chest. Unlike the others, he didn't look tired. He did, however, seem more than ready to end whatever it was they were caught up in.

"That's one thing we're looking into now," he said. "With the amount of Sleepers you were on, driving would have been almost impossible. But where your car was found was a good twenty miles from anything, and I've searched that road in both directions. There's no marks from running off the road or any kind of reckless driving."

Mel shared a look with Sterling.

"What are you saying?"

Detective Reiner actually shrugged.

"Either Ms. Blankenship here is one of those rare people who drive like a pro under the influence or—"

Mel was surprised she interrupted, but before she could stop herself she finished his thought.

"—or I wasn't the one driving."

Detective Reiner nodded.

Sterling wasn't a fan of the theory.

"So someone was driving her, drugged, to town and then—what?—was involved in a hit-and-run with Rose Simon's car before switching places with Mel and fleeing? It makes no sense."

Detective Lovett looked up at his colleague. Reiner answered.

"We're looking into the possibility that Jonathan Partridge might have been in the car with you."

It was like Sterling had been jolted awake. Mel wasn't far behind.

"Did you find him? Is he the one Brutus was chasing at the cabin?"

Reiner shook his head.

"The theme of this case is that we haven't found anyone. Yet. We're actually about to go to his house with a warrant. It doesn't take much for a judge to grant one for a Partridge."

Sterling had already told Mel about Jonathan's on-camera fight with Rose Simon before her murder, but she couldn't get her mind around him possibly being involved.

"Don't get me wrong, I am no fan of Jonathan's, but why do we think he's doing this, if he is? Revenge against me for not sticking up for his brother? Revenge for the fire? Why wait all these years?"

"You left."

Sterling's words were simple, blunt.

True.

Mel felt her face heat.

"Maybe he wanted you back in Kelby Creek," Sterling continued. "And maybe he finally found a way to do it. Just like with Rose."

A silence settled over them.

Mel didn't want to break it to say what she was thinking.

There was only one reason Mel would come back to Kelby Creek.

And he was sitting next to her.

"How does Ella fit into this?" she asked after the silence became too loud. "If this is revenge for his brother then, I guess, I get me and I get Rose. But why Ella? We talked earlier, and it seems like she's just some sweet girl who was visiting her grandmother and then woke up in a cabin next to me."

"We think she could have been taken on accident," Detective Lovett supplied. "Her grandmother lives a few miles from the cabin you were taken at. She might have been unlucky to see you being moved and was grabbed before she could call for help."

Mel was frustrated. It didn't help that she was starting to feel sick again.

"But why drug us, stick us in the cabin and then *leave* us? Why try to grab me at the Meeting House?" She balled the hospital sheet in her hands. "It just all sounds like bad planning, and I don't understand why. If this was really Jonathan, I can't imagine him being this *sloppy*."

She looked at Sterling for backup, but he stayed quiet.

Detectives Lovett and Reiner shared another look.

"We're still trying to figure out why you came back

to town." Reiner's voice was cold. Hard. Mel wasn't the only one frustrated and tired. "Why Rose's car was a part of your accident and then hours later, while you're in the hospital, she's killed and left in your home. Why after five years you show up with an address in your pocket that leads to the Meeting House, right to the people who want to take you. Why the man who showed up at that house had the weapon that killed Rose and, so far, an identity that is just as hard to pin down, as he might or might not ever wake from his coma. Why you were taken from a house in the aftermath of a tornado—was it planned for that night, or was the weather seen as an opportunity?—and why you were taken to a cabin, left alone and then able to escape, all while Jonathan Partridge has been missing for days now."

His voice had gone colder as he spoke. Sterling had become more tense.

"Okay, calm down there—" he started, but Reiner held up his hand in defense to cut him off.

He kept eye contact with Mel.

"I'm just trying to point out that this is not a normal investigation. We have a *backlog* of questions and, so far, less than a handful of answers. That's in large part because we have no idea how you fit into this. And, believe me, we're certainly trying to figure that, and everything else, out."

He stopped there. Then looked at Sterling.

Mel didn't need him to say it out loud, but she knew what he was thinking.

She was involved, and the only reason why her questioning had been the way it had was because of the deputy who wore a cowboy hat.

They trusted him.

He was vouching for her.

Even now she could see it in him, in the way his jaw was set, that he was ready to come out swinging.

Thankfully, Detective Lovett spoke with a cool tone.

"We can't get answers sitting in this room, so it's time for us to head out." He stood slowly. Then he extended a hand to both Sterling and Mel. "Rest," he implored them. "The mysteries of Kelby Creek are too strong for any one man or woman. We need all hands, and those hands are worthless to us if they're hurt and exhausted."

Sterling saw both men to the door.

Mel could read the tension in him without seeing how drawn his face was when he turned back to her. Again, Mel wanted to reach out to him—to embrace him and, maybe, kiss him just like she had before her memory had been blacked out—but another wave of exhaustion took over.

She closed her eyes against it, hoping the dizziness didn't show up again.

When she reopened them, she noticed Sterling had found his seat at her side.

That tension in him had lessened considerably.

"Foster's right. We need to get some rest and recoup."

Mel snorted.

"Every time I seem to open my eyes, I'm missing time and memory and am somewhere I'm not supposed to be. Maybe staying awake for once will do me some good."

It was meant as a joke—though there was some real fear there for Mel—but Sterling didn't find any humor in it.

His hand encircled hers. Together they rested next to her on the bed.

"This time will be different," he said, resolute.

"Why? Because drugging me hasn't worked out for whoever is behind this before, so they're probably done trying that trick?"

Sterling shook his head.

His voice dipped even lower. The deep sound rumbled through his hand and along her skin.

"Because, this time, I'm not leaving your side."

Chapter Fifteen

Mel dropped her suitcase to the living room floor and let out a cuss that was as loud as they came.

"Two. Days," she said, turning around to face Sterling. "Two long days in the hospital with nothing but time to try and figure out why I was in town, why Rose Simon came back and where Jonathan went and we got *nothing*. Nada. Zilch and zippo."

Mel had her hair back in a braid. It was messy but looked nice. All of her looked nice, in fact. Something Sterling had been worried about for the last two days. After Sam had gotten her and Ella to the hospital, Mel had become progressively worse until, finally, she'd gotten better. Little by little.

"I almost overdosed on an illegal street drug with a dumb name," she'd told him on the first night of him hovering. "I'm going to look and feel like a potato sack until it's all out."

She'd never looked like a potato sack—in Sterling's opinion, Mel could never look bad—but it was great to see her now with some color in her cheeks and some fire in her eyes. Waiting for that, and for her exhaustion to finally ebb, had put a stress in him that he'd hated to feel. It was only in her recovery that he'd let some of that worry go back to Brutus. Who wasn't doing as well.

He'd survived his surgeries, but he was far from out of the woods.

"There's nothing to do here," Marigold had told him before they'd left the hospital. "Go home. Everyone from the department will let you know the moment any one of us hears something."

So, Sterling had listened and brought a fired-up Mel in tow. Healed, hungry and ready to go, as per her own words.

"Just think of it as a testament to your skills in stealth," Sterling said. He dropped his hospital bag, courtesy of Sam, by the recliner. "Not even you could figure out what you were doing in hindsight. And you know you better than anyone else. That's skill."

It was just after lunch, and Sterling had already swung them into an unhealthy drive-through on the way home. They'd devoured tacos and theories on the ride over. Aside from the nitty-gritty of the mystery surrounding them, it had once again felt like old times—two teens dropping crumbs in the cab of his truck and shooting the breeze as they did it.

But they weren't teens anymore.

That was certainly apparent when the anger in Mel only grew.

"Well, I really wish I could go back and bonk myself on the head, because what a bunch of crap this has been. One minute I'm out there writing an article about patio furniture and the next I'm riding low on Sleepers and surrounded by people who have no idea what a whole group of *other* people are doing." She fell back into the couch with a loud sigh.

Sterling laughed.

It caught her attention. Her head popped up, hair from her braid escaping.

"And what's so funny? This has to be bothering you. Probably more than me! I mean, look at us. You help me, a tornado hits your house. You help me again, the poor sheriff has a heart attack." She disappeared from view. Sterling could hear her head hit the couch cushion. "I probably shouldn't be here lest I herald in the second coming of The Flood. Which, might I add, I'm pretty sure Cole Reiner thinks I'm trying to do. He can't get over the fact that I of all people am smack-dab in the middle of this."

She sighed again.

"Then again, if I wasn't me, I'd sure be suspicious. People already thought I was in cahoots with Rider. Once it gets out that I'm just casually where the action is, then it's game over for my already-crippled reputation with this town."

Mel finally had wound down. Sterling could hear it in her voice. She'd gone from fiery frustration all the way down to self-loathing.

Just as she had after Rider had gone to prison and Kelby Creek had turned on her.

Sterling hated hearing it again.

He might have had his own issues with Mel, but they were far outshone by his hatred for Rider Partridge. Mel might have chosen to marry him, but she hadn't chosen to be betrayed by him. To be strung up and tarred and feathered the way she had been.

"All right. All right." Sterling clapped his hands together. Mel's head popped up. He didn't answer her questioning eyebrow. Instead he went to the garage, found two old lounging chairs striped in pink and blue plastic, and passed her on the way to the back door.

The backyard wasn't large by any means, but it was private and, thanks to Sam's husband, now under the watchful eye of two of several security cameras set up around the house.

Sterling set up the first chair facing the back privacy fence and the second one right next to it. He didn't spell it out for Mel and sat down on his chair, taking his cowboy hat off in the process. His holstered gun, however, was firmly secured.

"Been a long time since we did this," Mel finally said. The squeak of her settling next to Sterling did something to him, but he wasn't going to think on it too much.

They'd both been through it within the span of a week.

He didn't always have to think about missing her.

"Remember the first time you made Sam and me do this?" he asked instead. "You said we needed to feed our leaves."

Mel laughed so hard and quickly that she snorted.

"Sam thought I was trying to get y'all to do some drugs, but all I was really doing was trying to make a clever joke about photosynthesis. Also, get a little bit of a tan. My legs were so pale that they were blinding me when we drove around in the car."

Sterling chuckled.

"Sam didn't last long, that much I remember about the first time we did it," he said.

Mel shook her head.

"After the way that boy complained about sweating, I was glad he decided to just let the two of us and these old loungers feed our leaves." Mel's voice changed so quickly that Sterling glanced over at her. She had her shoes off and pants rolled up. She ran her finger along the plastic at the side of her chair. "You kept these. The loungers."

There was something there—something in her words—that took a simple observation and made it punch well above its weight class.

It was appreciation and surprise and hurt and guilt and utter disbelief. Sterling knew it like he knew the sun on his skin was warm that Mel couldn't wrap her mind around someone holding on to something nice about her. Not when she was the ex-wife of Rider Partridge, the connected corruptor of Kelby Creek.

It was easy to blame and be angry at Mel for leaving him—God knew it had still been sitting heavy on his chest—but right then and there, Sterling was listening to a woman who had disappeared on him and finally hearing something else.

A woman who didn't think she was worth saving a good memory for.

And so Sterling did something he hadn't planned on doing.

He let it go.

He let it all go right then and there.

He forgave Mel for leaving, he forgave her for staying away and he forgave her for being the only woman he'd ever truly loved because, in the end, he couldn't blame her for being the perfect woman for him.

She just was.

Sterling went back to staring at the fence and took a deep breath. He ran his thumb over the brim of his cowboy hat and let that breath out.

Forgiving her wasn't just thinking it, so Sterling answered a question he should have already answered before.

"Dad made space for me in the garage when I left Kelby Creek," he started. "Just for the stuff that wasn't as easy to tote around. When I first set out, I only really had a few bags of stuff, which worked out well for me, since I went to Florida." Mel was keeping quiet, but he knew she was surprised at that. Florida had never been a place Sterling was keen on.

"I ended up staying with my cousin Joseph in an apartment near the beach and working a construction job with him. After The Flood, believe it or not, even if you came out squeaky-clean with the investigations, it was a pain just to get a law enforcement interview. So, I helped build fancy houses for a year instead."

He laughed because it was still funny to him now.

"Then Joseph went and married a client, which made the boss mad, and we both got canned. I couldn't be too mad at it since he made me his best man, but I didn't have much fun looking for a new place to live and work." He leaned back and changed his view to the blue sky.

"So I left the sun and sand for the dreariest place I've ever lived, out in Tennessee for a spell. Smaller town than Kelby Creek and, honestly, kind of weird, but I stayed there doing odd jobs for another year. May have been because of a lady I started dating, though. Her name was Rhonda, and she made a mean cup of coffee. Wasn't meant to be, though. We broke up and then I finally made my way to Georgia."

Sterling shrugged and stepped over the real reason he'd broken up with Rhonda and got to the end of his five years away from Mel. "A sheriff from a county triple the size of Dawn County offered me a job. She was a good woman, smart and a fighter. Newly elected and out there trying to make her hometown a better place, no matter who tried to get in her way. One day we were sitting around the break room table when a news story from Kelby Creek came in. It was a good story, and the reporter made a comment that maybe Kelby Creek was finally putting some good out into the world."

Sterling thumped his hat with his finger.

"And that burned a hole through me," he said. "There I was in Georgia, missing the struggle of my home trying to become better. To *be* better. And the sheriff saw that and told me that the job was a fight and to leave only if I was willing to fight it. So, I came home, got this place and have been here ever since."

That was it.

That was his last five years summed up.

Sterling took his cowboy hat and put it on. Mel took a few seconds before she spoke.

"And you brought the loungers here."

He nodded.

"Nothing else I'd rather feed my leaves on."

Sterling didn't know what to expect, but Mel falling into a laughing fit was a sound he more than liked.

"Wow. That really *does* sound like some kind of euphemism for doing drugs. No wonder Sam was so squirrelly about it when I first asked."

Sterling joined in.

MEL WAS WARM that night after her shower. It took a bit to realize that their session in the sun had more to do with it than the thoughts she'd been having about Sterling in said shower.

Her cheeks were rosy, along with her arms. She had a little sunburn going on, yet didn't much mind it.

Not after what else had gone on while she earned the slight heat of the burn.

Something had shifted between her and Sterling, and she had no idea what had been the cause. Not only had he told her about the years of his life that she'd missed, their conversation had been easier after. They'd talked about a lot and also nothing all at the same time. Which was fine by Mel. She'd forgotten how great it felt to just *be* with someone.

And that someone being Sterling Costner?

Mel looked at her reflection in the mirror. She was smiling.

Maybe it was time.

Maybe it was *finally* time to tell him.

To explain why she'd gone the way she had. Why she'd just left.

Why she'd never planned on coming back.

Because, really, she'd stayed away for years, and now she was back because of the bad.

What would be the harm of telling him now?

Rider.

It was an automatic response with years of practice.

Mel's head hurt at how loud one name within her mind could be.

But there it was.

There *he* was.

Just as he had been at the courthouse that day five years ago.

Mel hated remembering her ex-husband's sneer as he gave her one last parting speech.

"Sterling Costner is as good as in a prison cell right next to me as long as you stay with him. All it would take was a few words from me to a few people." Rider had leaned in close, his lawyer letting the close contact happen, knowing there would be no repercussions for him. *"And before you remind me that I'm going to prison, let me remind you, my dear sweet Melanie, that I helped destroy an entire town from the comfort of our living room. Imagine what I could do to one single man with nothing more than my righteous anger to keep me company all day, every day."*

Mel watched her smile fade in the mirror.

Their marriage might have been a lie, but Mel had recognized that threat for what it was.

The absolute truth.

Being with Sterling wasn't dangerous for her. It was dangerous for him.

If Rider knew she was here now?

Mel turned away from the mirror.

She was angry.

She wished Rider would have just used his power to attack her, not threaten the people she loved.

Mel let her new anger and frustration lead her into the guest bedroom to change. Marigold, who had spent a portion of time after her shift in the hospital room with them trying to find *something* to help them sort everything out, had been kind enough to go clothes shopping for her, since Mel had only packed for what looked like two to three days. She absently slid into a brand-new matching pajama short set and then went to braiding her wet hair.

Sterling could be heard walking around the kitchen, the hallway, his room. Ambling through the house, trying to get them answers without leaving her side to do so. Trying to keep her safe despite all evidence making her seem like the one who was actually making everything happen.

He was a good man.

A great man.

Someone who deserved a great woman who didn't always find herself in the thick of bad, bad things.

Mel let her wet braid drop across her shoulder. The water started to spread through the fabric of her shirt.

With a fire that burned quick and hot through her heart, Mel wished she'd never met Rider Partridge.

Then, with a scorched heart that turned heavy as quickly as it had burned, Mel felt the real truth she'd been avoiding settle.

She should have never married Rider.

And now the man she should have was paying for her mistake.

Chapter Sixteen

The house was quiet.

Mel was not.

Sterling was in his bed, door open to the hallway, gun on his nightstand and his phone fully charged. Along with the security footage application that was currently monitoring the outside of his house...that he had already looked at several times, since sleep wasn't coming easy.

Judging by the constant movement he heard coming from the guest bedroom, he wasn't the only one.

It wasn't until eleven rolled around that Mel admitted defeat. Her door opened slowly. When she saw him sitting up, lights still on, she gave him a small smile.

"I think I've gotten used to hospital machines beeping and nurses waking me up every two hours," she said in greeting. "Every time I drift off, I jolt awake trying to figure out where I am and where my IV pole is."

"I could sit by your bed and try to make the beeping sounds," he offered. "I'm not sure we should try and replicate the IV part, though. I might deal well with a lot of things, but the last time I had an IV put in my arm and watched, I almost passed out."

He set his phone aside and waved her in.

Mel cocked her head to the side slightly.

"When's the last time you had an IV put in?"

Sterling snorted.

"The last time someone tried to use me as a pincushion."

He lifted his shirt and turned. The exposed skin on his side and beneath his rib cage had a nasty scar across it. Mel came closer.

"Twelve stitches and several 'you're lucky' comments from the ER staff," he continued. "It happened when I was in Georgia and on a call for the department. Let's just say that I met a very unhappy customer who was, thankfully, not as good with his aim with a knife as he was at being drunk and disorderly."

Mel wasn't a fan. She surveyed the scar up close. Sterling could smell his extra body wash from the guest bathroom wafting off her.

"I know we haven't seen each other for five years, but it's still wild to see the reminders," she said after a moment. "Mind some company?"

Sterling patted the spot next to him in bed.

Mel went around to the other side and climbed in. He was surprised to see her slip under the covers, but, then again, he had the house's AC set to slight winter. The temperature outside might have cooled off, but that just meant the humidity was now out in fine fashion. Mel's legs slid across the sheets, a few inches from his own.

As he did with the scent of his body wash, Sterling tried to rein in his focus and ignore the new closeness.

"Not bad for a brand-new mattress someone else picked out." Mel bounced a little. "I'm a little jealous, to be honest. The mattress I have back at my apartment needs to be hauled off to a dumpster and dealt a killing hand. The poor thing was cheap when I got it and had to endure several moves after. Also a stint of time with my past roommate's cat, Busta Rhymes."

Sterling laughed at that. It egged Mel on. She slapped lightly at his shoulder.

"See? That's how you accurately respond to learning Busta Rhymes's name," she said. "When I first heard it and laughed, my roommate called me rude!"

"I would think *not* reacting to his name would have been the ruder thing to do. I mean, you just don't name your cat that and expect people to not say anything and just nod."

Mel nodded with enthusiasm.

"Exactly!" Sterling repeated the name with another long laugh. Mel was grinning ear to ear. "Glad you enjoy that as much as I did when I heard it the first time, because I will, one hundred percent, name my dog that. Just as soon as I adopt him or her."

Her words were resolute.

So much so in fact that they changed the direction of the conversation.

"Is that what you'll do when you go back? To Birmingham." Sterling was genuinely curious, yet he couldn't deny his words held a weight. Sure, they'd started talking about their past, but they hadn't for a moment talked about the future. "When this is all over, I mean."

It was like they were outside again. Both looked straight ahead as they spoke.

"I don't know," Mel answered. "With everything going on here—with me stuck in this weird web and looking like the one who's at the center of it—it's hard to even think about what's next. I already had to call my boss and take a leave of absence. My job might not be the hardest thing to do in the world, but the need to focus is definitely still there…and I'm definitely having a hard time with that."

She sighed and slid down a little, farther into the bed.

"A part of me wishes I could live two lives," she continued. "One of them could be me going back to my small apartment, adopting a dog, going to the gym and being a loner until I want to be social again. No muss, no fuss. But the other life? The other me? She could do better here. She could figure out what's going on and make peace with this town. Make them see I'm not the bad guy they've always wanted me to be. Then— Well, then they would believe what *I* say. Not whatever Rider Partridge might say to hurt me."

Sterling felt his eyebrow raise at that.

"What do you mean, whatever Rider Partridge *might* say?"

It was a small movement, but Sterling watched Mel tense. She shrugged into it.

"I'm just tired of being a walking reminder of Kelby Creek's long-standing wound," she fielded. "If I'm going to be remembered for something in this town, I'd sure like to *not* be the villain."

Sterling opened his mouth to tell Mel that she *wasn't* anyone's villain, but his phone went off, vibrating across his nightstand.

Mel sat at attention. Her hair brushed against his arm as she tried to look around him at the phone's screen.

"Who is it? Detective Lovett?"

Sterling felt a small jab of guilt.

"No. It's Dad. I forgot to call him after we got out of the hospital." Sterling started to get out of bed. Mel, too. He held out his hand to stop her. "I don't mind you staying. I'll only be a sec."

He took the call with him out into the living room, and Mel must have listened. Sterling never heard her pad across the hallway to the guest bedroom and, after taking longer than he intended with his call before ending it, he walked back to see the door still open.

Then he turned to his room.

And there she was.

Right where he left her, eyes closed and face lax with sleep.

Sterling stayed his feet for just a spell and took in the sight.

"I'm a reminder. A walking, talking reminder that not all wounds are made by weapons and bad people. Sometimes they're made by people trying to pretend that everything is okay."

He heard her words from the day out at the field, slushies in each of their hands.

Everything wasn't okay.

But, for the briefest of moments, Sterling decided to pretend like it was.

Everything was warm.

Mel kept her eyes closed but stretched wide.

She felt good. Better than she had in a while.

That feeling went away in a flash. Mel opened her eyes as something moved next to her.

Rather, someone.

The warmth she was feeling was a man. A man she was draped over, head against his shoulder, chest against his side.

Adrenaline shot through Mel. She forgot where she was, fear blinding her.

Then that person moved again. The arm he had wrapped around her tightened its hold.

Mel's racing heart started to slow.

She smelled the woods and pine and spice.

The same body wash she'd used on her body.

Sterling.

Mel lifted her cheek gently.

They were in Sterling's bed—she must have fallen asleep—and the man of the hour was right there with her. His eyes were closed, still asleep. Mel's face heated as she realized just how close they were. She had no doubt it had been her doing. When they'd been together before, she'd been notorious for leaving her side of the bed and wrapping herself around the man. Even in sleep she felt comforted by him.

And even in his sleep, he'd always found a way to wrap her up—to keep her safe.

Mel wished she could stay like that a bit longer, but something had woken her up.

She stilled herself, waiting, before his cell phone went off again.

This time the man woke up. He met her gaze before gently untangling himself.

Mel's face was aflame, but she didn't comment on their compromising position.

She wanted to know why someone was calling when it looked like the sun had barely come up through the crack in the blinds over the new window.

"Costner." Sterling cleared his throat. He sat up, running a hand down his face. Mel could hear a man's voice but couldn't recognize it.

Which she didn't like, considering how Sterling sat up ramrod straight after whatever it was the man said.

"Are you kidding me?" he asked, voice filled with anger.

He was out of bed in one fluid movement.

Mel followed, body still wobbling from sleep.

Whoever was on the phone was talking fast.

Sterling was at his dresser, grabbing a pair of jeans while he listened.

Mel tried to catch his gaze to mouth a question, but he kept moving.

"You know that's a bunch of crap. There's no way," he continued.

Mel ducked to the side, trying to meet his eye again. It only worked when the doorbell rang.

Sterling ended the call, no goodbye to the other party.

"What's going on?" Mel asked.

Sterling's voice was low, only a bit above a growl.

"Go get dressed. I'll take care of this."

Mel wanted more than that but listened.

She hurried across the hall to the guest bedroom

while Sterling threw on a shirt. Mel listened to him stomping down the hallway to the front door as she changed and used the bathroom in record time.

It turned out, maybe she should have taken her time.

"This is insane," she heard Sterling almost yelling when she made it to the living room. Her stomach dropped at what she walked into.

A Dawn County Sheriff's Department deputy was standing next to a very intense-looking Detective Cole Reiner. His badge was hanging around his neck. His lips were pulled down in a frown.

"This is what's happening," Reiner said, resolute. "And if you try to stop it, you'll only make everything worse for *both* of you."

Sterling finally noticed she'd come in the room. He turned to Mel with nothing but fire in his words.

"I'm not going to let this happen."

On reflex alone Mel touched Sterling's arm. It seemed to stay his rising rage.

She looked to Reiner next.

"Not going to let *what* happen?"

The detective, to his credit, didn't look happy saying his answer. Still, he said it all the same.

"Ella Cochlin came to the department this morning and recanted her original statement of not remembering what happened to the two of you." He glanced at Sterling. It was only for a second, but Mel knew then where this was headed. "Ms. Cochlin said that *you* were the one who attacked and drugged her outside her grandmother's cabin while she was out on an early-morning jog. And that your partner drugged you to make it look like you were the victim."

Mel's mouth was hanging open. She felt like she was dreaming again.

"What?" Her voice pitched high, even to her own ears. "*I* attacked and drugged her? That makes no sense. I was the one who was here one minute, then in a cabin hours later. How did she even remember? I haven't been able to recall either time. And who the heck is my partner? Sterling? That's a big side of 'I don't think so.'"

Sterling didn't add on to her questions. She realized it was because he'd probably already asked them himself.

Reiner answered, regardless.

"Ms. Cochlin had far less of the drug in her system. The doctors say she stood a better chance of remembering something. As for the why, we're still looking into that, but I personally think it might have to do with your partner."

Mel gave Sterling an incredulous stare.

"They said that Ella found her phone on her running route near the fisherman's cabin," he explained. "They said there's a picture on it of you, time-stamped early Monday morning. Talking to Jonathan Partridge."

"An hour before your car accident, several before Rose Simon's murder and—may I add—in between those two incidents he also came to visit you in the hospital," Reiner added. "Do you have anything to say about that?"

All eyes went to Mel.

She had nothing to say.

No answers to give.

She was speechless.

Sterling was not.

"Something is going on, but she isn't a part of this, Reiner. You know that."

The detective shook his head.

"What I know is that every lead we've gotten goes right back to her." Reiner addressed Mel directly now. "To you. So I'm going to need you to come to the department with me now. And, if you don't come willingly, then you'll come in handcuffs." He nodded to the deputy at his shoulder.

"Your choice."

Chapter Seventeen

The handcuffs never went on, but Mel got into the back of the sheriff's deputy SUV all the same. A feat considering how riled up Sterling was. He tried to convince Detective Reiner and the deputy that they were wrong up until they started driving to the department.

That Mel hadn't attacked Ella. That she hadn't drugged herself.

That she hadn't had anything to do with Rose Simon's murder.

But his words got lost in the heat of the day.

"I'll meet you at the station," he called out before the door shut behind her.

Mel nodded to him. She felt numb.

And not because she was surprised, but because she couldn't help but wonder…was she the villain after all?

Detective Reiner was texting someone from the passenger's seat.

"If I were you, I'd stop letting Deputy Costner throw himself in front of you," he said, gaze still fixed to his phone. "Just tell the truth and cooperate and we can minimize the fallout as much as possible."

Mel didn't like that.

"I am telling the truth and I will cooperate," she said hotly. "But I'm telling you that this is all some wild misunderstanding. If I really was photographed with Jonathan Partridge, then something else must be going on. *He* must be behind it. Because he's definitely not my partner in crime. I mean, you do know about what happened to him, right? About the fire?"

Reiner nodded. His head was still angled down at his phone. It incensed her, so she continued, trying even more desperately to make her point.

"When the investigation into The Flood turned to Rider, he was given a heads-up that a search warrant was issued for his office half an hour before it was executed. I overheard him make plans to try and go out there and I warned the department before he could destroy any evidence. What I didn't know was that Jonathan was already there and half the office was on fire. Jonathan was caught trying to save some documents and got burned because of it. He blames *me* for the pain and scars and helping the town tar and feather his brother's good image. He said if I'd only stood up for Rider, if I hadn't helped go after him, then everything would have played out differently."

"But you didn't start the fire," Reiner pointed out. "Neither did he. It was an employee of Rider Partridge. One who didn't know Jonathan was inside, last I heard."

Mel shook her head. She crossed her arms over her seat belt.

"It didn't matter," Mel said. "Jonathan placed blame on me because I didn't do one thing to stop the stone rolling down the hill once it had been pushed. Everything after was my fault. Including a fire I never even saw because I was in FBI custody."

They were out of the neighborhood now and heading toward the other side of town. Instead of going through it to the department, the deputy took the county road that went around. Probably to keep Sterling from getting on their tail when he finally hit the road behind them.

"What happened in the past, fire or not, doesn't change what's happening now." Reiner finally put down his phone. He turned to look at her. "You will have the time and more than the opportunity to tell your side of this story. Just like Ella. Just like Jonathan when we find him. Even Sterling is going to get his fair share. We're going to figure this out, one way or the other."

Mel wanted to say more, but what words could really sway the man? Especially if she herself was questioning everything?

So she quieted.

Reiner turned back around in his seat.

Mel wished she were back in bed, warm against Sterling and torn between her desire to stay with him and go back to her life.

But Kelby Creek was proving to be wholly unkind.

"Wait, why are we out here, James?" Reiner made a show of looking this way and that out the window. "Pretty sure this is going to add fifteen minutes onto our—"

Mel saw the car before Reiner did and screamed.

It swerved from the other lane of traffic and went right at the passenger's side.

The impact happened in a blink. Mel's adrenaline and fear surged as she was thrown forward and back by whiplash. The airbags deployed, and a scattering of dust from them was floating in the air when everything stopped. The nasty sounds of whirling car parts and metal settling into places it shouldn't be filled the world around her.

Mel touched her head. The scab from her first accident was gone.

This time she was just shaken, not hurt.

At least she didn't think she was.

The front of the SUV was undeniably bent, but her cage in the back was intact.

Mel unbuckled her seat belt. She needed to help the deputy and detective.

The man known as James was the only one moving.

"Are you okay?" she asked. "Is Detective Reiner?"

James grunted. He opened his door with ease and without a verbal answer. Mel expected him to call for backup or go to the passenger's side or just go check on the other car.

He didn't.

Instead he opened the door next to her.

"Get out." Blood was coming from his busted lip, but his words were clear.

"I don't understand—"

"Get. Out."

James grabbed Mel by the wrist and yanked her out of the SUV in one quick movement. It was one thing to be treated poorly because of public opinion—it was another to be manhandled after a car accident because you weren't liked.

Mel was about to put that into words after insisting they check on Reiner when she finally took a look at the second car.

The driver was already out and walking toward them.

Mel recognized him instantly.

It was the man from the Meeting House.

He had a gun in his hand.

And his eyes focused on James.

"You ready? We don't have long," he said.

James nodded.

Mel started to back up but stilled in mute horror as James pulled his service weapon from his holster.

Then gave it to her.

Mel took it on reflex, just as she yelped when James took it back. He handed it to the new man, who put it in the waist of his pants. Then James lay down on the ground next to the opened back door. He nodded to the other man.

Mel watched in horror as the man from the Meeting House backed up, took aim and shot James in the chest.

James made an awful noise.

Then the man switched the gun's aim to her.

"Now get in the car or you're next."

Mel didn't move. The man switched his aim again.

This time it was on the front passenger's seat.

"Do as I say or the detective isn't waking up."

Mel looked at Reiner. He still hadn't moved.

Then she looked at the open road behind them.

It was empty.

Part of her wished she'd seen Sterling there, ready to attack.

Part of her was glad he wasn't behind them.

"Okay." Mel nodded. "I'll go."

The other vehicle was an aged blue Bronco. It had damage from ramming the deputy's SUV but not enough to make a difference.

"I don't understand." He pushed her through the driver's side door and across the seat to the passenger's side. He grunted at the effort. "Why are you doing this?"

The man looked worse for wear. He was wearing a button-up, open at the top, and cargo shorts. He shouldn't have been sweating as badly as he was, yet he was drenched.

Mel would bet it had something to do with the fact that thick bandages could been seen through his open shirt.

And the fact that Sterling had shot him.

Twice.

He kept his mouth closed and focused on keeping the gun aimed at her while he put the vehicle in Drive. Mel contemplated trying to crash the car as they picked up speed.

She decided to wait.

She might survive a car crash, but she wasn't confident she could survive a bullet to the belly. He had already shot at her before. What was stopping him from pulling the trigger if she fought back?

"Just tell me *something*," Mel tried again when he didn't speak. The car lurched onto the road but drove fine after. She gave James and Detective Reiner one last look. Reiner still hadn't moved. James had now joined him in that state. "Like why did you shoot him? Why do you want me? *What's going on?*"

All the frustration boiled over into her last question. It came out less of a scared wobble and more of an angry confusion.

It caught the man off guard.

He shook the gun at her, then went back to looking at the road.

"Don't go getting no ideas," he warned. "You won't get answers from me, so you might as well just wait to ask the man in charge."

Mel would have shaken the man had she been able.

"*Who* is in charge and *of what*?"

The man shook his head this time.

"You really don't remember nothing, do you?" He chuckled. It obviously pained him. "I took some Sleepers once, and all I did was hallucinate that the world had flipped upside down. I guess everyone gets hit by them a bit different."

He took an upcoming turn that would point them back to the heart of town instead of near the department. In the process he gave her a quick sidelong look.

"You don't remember seeing him? Talking to him?"

"Him?" Mel's voice broke on the one syllable.

The man gave her a pained smirk.

"I'm not about to ruin the surprise. Plus, it's not part of his plan for me to even talk to you right now." Mel jumped as he took his hand off the steering wheel and then hit the same wheel hard. It made the vehicle swerve a little. "I took two shots and was lying there dying and still I have to make up for messing up the first plan.

'Don't hurt, shoot or kill Melanie Blankenship.'" He blew out a breath. Then started cursing.

"I'd ask what makes you so special, but I'm guessing it's not about you," he continued, very chatty for a man who'd just said he wasn't supposed to be talking at all. "You know, I'd feel sorry for you if I had half a mind to. But I don't." He shrugged. "All I gotta say is you sure know how to pick 'em."

That cold sense of dread that had been building was body-chilling now.

Mel didn't remember what had happened during her Sleepers-induced memory loss, but she had the horrible feeling that she knew who he was talking about.

And it wasn't Jonathan.

"Now I'm going to shut my trap and keep driving," the man went on. His voice dropped low. He shook the gun again. "And if you ask me one more question, I might just pull this trigger, then put my foot to the floor and leave this horrible little town behind. Consequences be damned. Got it?"

Mel felt numb.

She didn't understand.

And, for the first time, she didn't want to anymore.

She kept quiet.

Though not even that lasted long.

They pulled in behind a building near downtown Kelby Creek. It looked nice, even though a For Sale sign was in the street-facing window.

"Why are we here?"

The man killed the engine. Beads of sweat dotted his forehead.

"Just one thing to do before we head out."

He had them in the alley behind the for-sale building, facing the sidewalk. A few blocks up was the official downtown.

Mel didn't understand.

Then she saw her.

A woman walked across the sidewalk in front of them, grocery bags in hand.

The man next to Mel was fast.

He was out of the vehicle, gun drawn.

Mel realized three things all together.

The gun he drew wasn't the one he'd had pointed at her. It was James's gun.

The woman wasn't a stranger. It was Ella Cochlin.

Then, when the man shot Ella and she crumpled to the ground, groceries spilling across the sidewalk around her, there was a third and sudden realization. One that made Mel realize there was one theory she'd been dancing around but hadn't yet entertained.

The man hurried back, jumped in the driver's seat and had him and Mel going back out the way they'd come.

Mel refused to say a word.

She was in shock. She was crying.

She was trying to work out a way from the new hell she'd found herself in.

Because, even though she didn't have all the answers, she finally understood one horrible fact.

She *was* the villain.

Chapter Eighteen

Sterling knew something was wrong the moment his feet hit the parking lot of the sheriff's department.

And not just the obvious.

That much was clear the second Marigold met him at his truck. She was in her street wear but had her badge on her hip. There was an excitement about her and not at all one that was good. There was also an undeniable amount of relief that followed. She didn't waste time on any greeting.

"Half the people in that building thought you might not show," she bowled into him with. "I told them you aren't like that. You're a good one, but I'll tell you, it sure feels good that you didn't prove me a liar."

Sterling didn't understand.

"Of course I'd show," he said, indignant that anyone would think otherwise. "After Reiner took Mel in like that, you better believe I'm going to come defend her. This is ridiculous. Mel—"

"—is missing," Marigold interrupted.

Sterling paused. It didn't last long.

"What? She just left my house with Reiner a few minutes ago."

Marigold shook her head but didn't explain.

"Did you follow them here? Did you see them at all on the road after they left?"

Sterling hated to shake his head.

"No. I—I had to change and grab my holster and badge." He motioned to his service weapon. His cowboy hat, the one that made him feel mighty, was atop his head. "But I was maybe three minutes behind."

"Well, a lot happened in those three minutes."

"Explain."

Sterling didn't mean to be curt, but he definitely wasn't trying to be polite. Not when the stakes suddenly felt like they were rising even higher than when Mel had left at the threat of handcuffs.

"Park just responded to a Good Samaritan call about a wreck and shooting out on County Road 12."

Sterling opened his mouth, adrenaline surging, but she was quick to hurry on. "He found Deputy Reynolds's cruiser with an unconscious Cole in the front seat and a shot Reynolds lying on the road. Next to an opened back door. Mel wasn't there."

That adrenaline rerouted from dread to hope.

The change wasn't lost on Marigold.

"And that's the problem, Sterling," she added. "Reynolds was responsive when Park was calling in an ambulance. He said someone rammed them off the road. And then forced him to let Mel out."

Sterling shook his head. That hope disappeared at the movement.

"So she's been taken. Again," he growled out. Anger was instant. He shouldn't have let Reiner take her. "We have to—"

Marigold did something that she had never done before during their time as partners. She placed a hand gently on his chest. The contact stilled him.

"Sterling, Deputy Reynolds said the gunman was Jonathan Partridge…and that he was working *with* Mel to help her escape. She even took Reynolds's gun before getting into the other car."

Sterling was already shaking his head.

"No way did Mel have anything to do with this. No way she's working with Jonathan. Deputy Reynolds has it wrong."

"He's got a bullet in him. And Mel was being brought in as the lead suspect for conspiracy."

"You don't believe me," Sterling said hotly.

It wasn't a question.

Marigold still answered.

"I trust your judgment and I trust your instinct," she said. "But even you have admitted that there was only one person in this world who ever truly blindsided you. And that was Mel when she left. Those were your words." Marigold took her hand back. "What makes you think this isn't the same thing? I mean, look at everything that's happened. How can anyone not think she's guilty? All roads point to her."

Sterling was ready to plead his case—that Mel wasn't a part of whatever was happening—but he stopped himself.

Mel *had* blindsided him when she'd left all those

years ago. And not because he was a man who thought he was so important that no one would ever leave him, but because he'd felt nothing but love from her. Even that morning before she'd left for the courthouse.

She'd woken up in his arms, chatted with him over coffee and then kissed him goodbye like they did every morning.

She'd even had plans with Sam for later in the week.

Then she was gone. All before he was even done with his shift.

Not a word in person. Just a text.

It hadn't made sense.

After being with her this past week, it made even less now.

Sterling felt something with her.

Just as he did then.

He felt love. He felt *her*.

And that's when it finally dawned on him.

"Then— Well, then they would believe what I say. Not whatever Rider Partridge might say to hurt me."

Sterling felt like an idiot.

Right then and there in the parking lot.

A downright fool.

Marigold's eyebrow rose.

"Is Foster here?" he asked, instead of explaining.

Marigold nodded.

"He was about to head to the hospital, though."

Sterling was off in a second.

"What? What's going on?" Marigold was hurrying behind him as he headed for the station doors, but Sterling's mind was running his own theories through the wringer.

It wasn't until he was inside the station and running

down the hall to Foster's office that he finally landed on something he should have realized years ago.

The door was open, and Sterling and Marigold rushed on in.

Foster stood behind his desk. His face was pinched. It only became worse when he saw Sterling. The look said it all.

Which was why Sterling put his hand up to stop his friend from saying whatever it was he was about to say.

"You're about to tell me that Mel is guilty of something new, aren't you? That after her daring escape from custody she's managed to do something else, right?"

Foster cocked his head to the side. His cell phone was in his hand at his side.

He nodded.

"Ella Cochlin was just shot downtown," he said. "A witness said they saw the same vehicle Deputy Reynolds described leaving the scene."

Sterling banged his fist on the desk.

"And I bet if we sit here long enough, something else will happen to point us right back to Mel."

Foster shared a look with Marigold.

Then the fates truly aligned. Foster's phone started ringing. He held up his finger.

"Don't move," he ordered. Then he answered the phone. "Detective Lovett."

Whoever was on the other end was talking fast. By Foster's responses, Sterling couldn't get a bead on what the call was about.

But then it ended and Foster's eyebrow was raised high.

"What are you getting at?" Foster asked.

Sterling swiped his cowboy hat off and pressed it into his chest. It was the only thing helping him remain focused on what was happening right now and not go running off to do a one-man search in his truck for Mel.

"There's only two options here," Sterling hurried. "The first is that Mel *is* guilty of whatever this is. That she came to town to partner up with Jonathan Partridge and kill Rose Simon for revenge or whatever working theory you might have. The second? That Mel is innocent, which is what I'm banking on, and if she is? Then why in the world does *every* single road lead back to her? Every single one of them, an almost-indisputable line between her and something wild."

Foster was thinking it through. Which meant that he hadn't completely given up on Mel yet.

So Sterling brought his point home.

"You said you checked in with the prison where Rider Partridge is being held to make sure everything is on the up and up, but are we sure it really is? Are we sure that Rider isn't the one doing what he has done best in the past?"

Foster glanced down at his phone.

He was still contemplating something, though his response was quick.

"That call was from Marco. He's at the hospital. The man you shot at the Meeting House woke up and has only said one thing since." Foster's eyes had widened. Excitement. But not the good kind, either.

Sterling could barely contain himself.

He knew in his heart that Mel was innocent. He just needed everyone else to get on board.

"What one thing?" he asked.

Foster shook his head in disbelief.

"That Rider Partridge was an innocent man."

MEL DIDN'T KNOW the house, but it was by the creek.

A wide one-story that was near the town limits. Not an ugly gray, not a place where fishermen hung their hats. A simple cabin with nice white trim and sky-blue paint on the siding.

And probably the place where she was going to die.

The man next to her parked at the back of the building. He'd grown awfully quiet the closer they'd come to the place. Now he took his sweet time staring at the back door.

Mel knew then, without a doubt, whom he was waiting for.

Still, she felt the cold creep up her spine as the door opened and the man of the hour stepped out.

Rider.

God bless him, he still looked good in a suit. And just as terrifying.

"We could go right now," Mel said into the quiet of the Bronco's cab. "We could leave long enough for the law to get him. I'd vouch for you. Say you saved me. That'll count."

The man pulled the keys from the ignition.

He almost looked sorry.

"We both know there's not much that man can't make happen. We leave now, he won't even have to lift a finger to catch us. He'll get someone else to do it for him."

Mel felt tears prick at her eyes.

Rider stood there, staring.

He knew that she knew.

"If I leave this car, he'll kill me," she said simply.

The man's answer was just as simple.

"If you *don't* leave this car, he'll kill *me*."

Mel let out a breath that shook and put her hand on the door handle.

In a moment of pure empathy, she paused.

"If I were you, once I get out of this car, I'd floor it out of here anyway," she said. "One thing Rider Partridge doesn't suffer is loose ends. That's why his brother has scars and he doesn't."

She didn't wait for a response.

Mel's shoes sank into the dirt of the drive. Rider stayed just where he was until she crossed the distance between them.

"I'm guessing we already did the whole 'nice to see you after all of these years' thing," she said in greeting. Mel was proud how her voice didn't shake. "But was it during the car accident or after the tornado?"

Rider was a study in contrasts to Sterling. She'd always known that, but right then and there, the details were glaring. Light hair, dark eyes and a body that was lean and short. Maybe that's why his suits meant so much to him. The same for his shiny shoes that cost more than most people's rent. He'd never be caught in worn clothes or family heirlooms. His hair never was tousled, and even now she could smell the expensive cologne he'd worn during their marriage.

It wasn't that Rider had expensive tastes.

It was that Rider didn't value anything else.

"After the tornado," he confirmed with a smirk. "But don't worry, the most we talked about was my insistence that it was better for everyone if you walked quietly to the car. Once we were in the car you, thankfully, became very quiet."

Mel had wondered why she would have left Sterling's house.

Now she knew.

Rider had threatened Sterling.

Of course he had.

"If you hadn't drugged me I would have asked why you were in Kelby Creek. Or, you know, not in prison."

Rider's smirk never wavered.

It made Mel's stomach knot.

His arrogance was only as powerful as his confidence, and both seemed to be in full swing. He stepped back into the house and waved her in.

"I have to wait for a package, and you know that I'm not a fan of humidity."

Mel glanced back at the Bronco.

Her friend had gotten out. Both guns in view.

She wasn't going to get far if she ran.

Not that running from Rider ever worked, apparently.

"Will I at least get some answers if I come inside?" she had to ask.

Rider laughed.

Once upon a time, that sound hadn't chilled her to the bone.

"Oh, don't worry, Melanie. You're going to get exactly what's coming to you."

Chapter Nineteen

Mel sat on a couch covered in an obnoxious floral print and, of all things, toucans. Rider sat across from her in an oversize armchair that was pastel blue.

It was almost comical.

Almost.

A man in fishing attire, complete with a mesh hat, stood in front of the windows that faced the main road. He gave them a half-hearted glance before returning his gaze out the window. On one hip he had a sheathed knife so big that it reached down to midthigh. Leaning against the other was a shotgun.

Rider didn't address the man. He knew Mel had seen him. Instead he crossed his ankle over his leg and threaded his fingers together over his knee. Calm. Confident.

Mel hated him.

"You look well, *Mel*," he started, laughing into his rhyme. That didn't last long. "I mean, I got worried there for a bit since you never visited me once during the last five years. Never mind you almost disappearing from the internet's radar. I actually lost you for a few weeks after you moved to Birmingham. By the way, can I say how glad I am that you finally got up the courage to rent your own apartment. Sure, sharing saves money, but you're only getting older, and a woman in her thirties with roommates sounds like a sad sitcom no one wants to watch."

Mel's jaw clenched.

She was angry.

She felt violated.

"Usually you don't keep tabs on your ex-spouse," she pointed out. "Especially when you weren't particularly there during the marriage. Never mind the fact that you're supposed to be in prison."

Rider scoffed. He was enjoying himself.

"Now, don't you go getting offended by the truth and then start telling lies to make yourself feel better." He leaned forward a bit and glazed right over her prison comment. "We both know you were happy during our marriage. The perfectly kept wife. Smiles aplenty, heart aflutter. Isn't that why this town turned on you so quickly? Your blindness? Your naivete? Your hope among hopes that the long hours I was pulling were for work and nothing more?" He shrugged. "Just because you say our marriage wasn't perfect, let me remind you that the divorce only came once the FBI did. It wasn't even on the table until then. Face it—you would have stayed with me till death did us part."

Mel felt heat crawl up from her belly and turn her face hot.

Rider knew he'd touched a big nerve.

He held up his hand to stop her from replying.

"Now, maybe I'm wrong. Maybe this town didn't turn on you simply because you married a charlatan. *Maybe* they turned on you because they knew that something was off about you. That you certainly couldn't *not* be involved." He smiled. It was genuine. "They're going to love finding out how right they were."

"You've been setting me up," Mel offered. Her voice had gone cold. Unfeeling. Stating facts since emotion wasn't going to get her anywhere with her sociopathic ex-husband. "You're making me the bad guy."

Rider held up his pointer finger.

"You *are* the bad guy. I'm just giving the town what they wanted five years ago—proof that they were right about you."

Mel shook her head.

"No one is going to believe this. I didn't do anything and I'm *not* going to do anything."

Rider laughed.

"You were on the way to the sheriff's department to get questioned by a very intense Cole Reiner. If our buddy Tate out there hadn't intervened, you'd be in an interrogation room. Again."

Mel wanted to point out that Sterling would have convinced them otherwise—that Mel was innocent—but Rider was already a step ahead.

"They might have believed Sterling's grand stand that he'd no doubt give to defend you, I'll give you that," he said. "But he's the only one who would do that. Which is why everything had to go to plan up until this moment. You leaving the love of your life out of the blue, with a text? Then no contact for five years? Kelby Creek already hated you, but doing that to a fine, country-fed Costner? A good man—a better man than you deserved?" Rider shook his head. "And then, as your final act in Kelby Creek, you're going to kill him? Any doubt left in their heads will fly out into the breeze."

Mel moved to the edge of her seat.

Her emotions broke through in a brilliant burst of fear.

"What do you mean, kill him?" Mel shook her head so hard her hair slapped her cheek. "You don't need to do this. You don't need to hurt him. Leave him out of this. You have me."

Rider uncrossed his legs. His hands went from threaded together to resting on each arm of the chair.

All humor was gone.

"I don't think you quite understand yet, but Sterling Costner is the *reason* I chose *you*."

He was transforming. From a gloating villain to his original title earned from The Flood. The Connected Corruptor. A man filled with charm and armed with patience. A man who was seeing his hard work finally pay off. It was Rider's turn for his voice to go void of emotion. Now, he was just stating facts.

"I was seventeen and interning with our family lawyer when I first realized that Kelby Creek was a double-sided coin," he continued. "The only person who ever won— who ever got anywhere they wanted—was the person who knew which side to call before a flip even happened. I wanted to be that person who knew the winning call before ever moving an inch. So, I was taught an invaluable lesson that I took to heart. Planning is power." A chill went up Mel's spine. He kept on. "It's painful, too. And, if you do it right, requires a lot of patience. Luckily, I have that in spades."

The man at the window moved. He looked down at his phone.

Rider paused to take in the movement, too.

He sat straighter.

Then his gaze was back on her.

"I knew eventually something would go wrong," Rider continued. "Whether on my end or someone else's. There's always going to be that unknown variable that has an unfortunate consequence. I realized that I needed a partner. And a patsy. So I asked you out on a date."

The chill across Mel spread and hardened.

"You married me so you could frame me, just in case?" Mel shook her head. She couldn't believe it.

Rider shrugged.

"It wasn't necessarily personal. I needed a type, and you fit it."

"A type?" Mel felt sick.

Rider might not have been the man she thought she'd married, but she never for a moment thought every single part of their relationship had been a lie.

He explained like the subject was as simple as apples and oranges.

"Someone pretty, smart and capable," he said. "Someone who's also quiet, somewhat a mystery. They're not close with the family they had growing up so they're left craving to create their own. They're nice and ready to sacrifice if needed, but there's only really one or two people that they'd burn the world down for. Bonus points if one of those people happen to be well-liked or beloved by many." Rider held his hands out to motion to her. "And then there you were. Quiet unless pushed, parents detached, notable in public and wildly in love with a town favorite."

"Sterling."

"Sterling Costner. Bless the both of you for not waiting too long after my arrest to finally act on your feelings. Also, bless you both for not keeping it a secret."

Mel hung her head a little. She looked at her hands but was remembering the past.

"You threatened Sterling so I'd leave him in the dust and everyone would know it. You got me to hurt a good man because you knew it would only make Kelby Creek hate me more."

Rider clapped his hands.

"And *that's* why poor Deputy Costner is about to have a very bad day. If you kill him? Your one true defender, a man who's been in love with you since you were teens, then there's nothing you can say that will change anyone's mind. Not with everything else I've planned."

Mel opened her mouth—she didn't know what she was going to say. She didn't understand everything that Rider had done or was doing. She was missing pieces of his clearly elaborate puzzle. But, lucky for her, Rider loved the sound of his own voice.

He stood, shared another look with the man at the window. He faced her again.

"The moment the mayor was suspected of being connected to Annie McHale's abduction was the moment I started planning on how to get out of prison. How to stay out once everyone figures out I had escaped." He lowered himself, bending over and using the couch cushions to prop himself up over her. Mel fought the urge to headbutt him. She fought the urge to yell, too. "Patience is a virtue. Planning is power. And you, my dear, are about to be revealed as the actual Connected Corruptor and the reason why Annie McHale was really in our basement. All because I'm so damn good at both."

Rider rose. This time he spoke to the man at the window.

"Time for a ride."

THE BASEMENT WAS UNRECOGNIZABLE. Just as it was unavoidable.

Like everything about Mel's relationship with Rider, something became apparent about it and the house it was beneath. But only in hindsight.

"That's why you left me this place," Mel said. "Another way to damn me down the line."

Rider hadn't monologued on the drive over. He'd spoken in hushed words to the man with the fisherman's hat, but Mel hadn't understood them. Just the gun in the man's hands.

Now they were back at the house.

Rider Partridge's castle.

He was smiling.

"When you didn't even try to sell it—which would

have been met with so many issues that it would have looked like you weren't trying to sell it at all—I had me a party in prison. I'm assuming not many people understand why you held on to this place. It definitely doesn't help public opinion of you."

He motioned to the area around them.

In what had once been a basement filled with a swarm of FBI agents, and at one point Annie McHale, there was now a cold quiet. Several boxes were stacked high across the tile floor while a chair sat stationary against the wall.

"When did you get all of these boxes in?" Mel had to ask. She answered herself before he could. "The tornado. The power was out across this side of town for hours. That's why I didn't get an alert for the security system."

Rider nodded.

"You actually were out in the car while some of this was being moved inside. Unconscious, but I had you sitting up in full view. Constance McCarthy glanced your way when she was hustling by with that yappy dog of hers—can't believe she's still around, to be honest—but I'm not sure she realizes yet that it was you. She'll probably put two and two together later. Just another dash of suspicion to put on you for Kelby Creek."

Mel walked up to the nearest box. It wasn't like an Amazon package or a box you'd get from the FedEx store to move. It was perfectly square, taped up neatly and void of any markings. Rider let her open the closest one.

Her already-knotted stomach tightened.

There was a case of plastic syringes inside. Too many. Vials lined the bottom, along with plastic bands.

"Drugs. Sleepers, I'm assuming."

Rider laughed.

"You sure pick up on things fast." He slapped the corner of the box. "It's hard to sell so many people on the idea that *you* were the one pulling all the strings involving my shenanigans back in the day without a few current shenanigans. Plus, Sleepers can be addictive, and you've had more than your fair share in your system twice now."

He moved her from the stack of boxes, around a few more and to a chair positioned at the back of the room. It was from upstairs, bought months before The Flood and never used after. Lavender cloth, wooden arms and polished legs. There were handcuffs around each side. Rider maneuvered her to sit down. He cuffed her left wrist but not her right.

"Wouldn't it have been easier to just do this?" Mel was back to fighting tears. She was tired. "To just plant something on me? Heck, wouldn't have killing me been easier?"

She hated to say it, but she felt it in her soul.

"Couldn't you have escaped and disappeared and never looked back?"

He checked that her handcuff was secure.

"I may be a patient man, but that doesn't mean I'm going to let my entire reputation be permanently destroyed. So, I spun a web and made you the spider. Making me one of several flies haplessly caught."

Mel continued to hold back her tears.

"Our entire relationship was a lie. None of it meant anything to you."

Mel knew she shouldn't have cared, but at the moment she let the hurt in.

"I thought we were happy at one point," she continued. "We laughed and kissed and took goofy pictures on our honeymoon. I have *good* memories with you, Rider. Honestly good ones."

He crouched in front of her, smile back in place. His gloved hand was soft as it brushed a strand of her hair behind her ear.

"Oh, my Melanie." There was an almost imperceptible shake of his head. "You were a plan."

Rider pulled something from his pocket.

It was a ring, but not her old one.

It was simple and gold and pretty.

"The only man who ever wanted to marry you for something as trivial as love never gave this to you."

Mel felt her eyes widen.

It made Rider all the happier.

"You found this in Sterling's things after the tornado. You put it on and were smiling when I showed up. My guess is it was meant for you, but, well, you know, you left the poor sap, heart in his hand."

He took her right hand and slipped the ring onto her fourth finger.

The fit was perfect.

"Such a shame," Rider said. "In another life you and Sterling might have made it."

He stood and walked to the bottom steps in the most dramatic fashion yet.

"Don't go anywhere. We still have some things to discuss. But first, I need to get some incentive for you."

He didn't say anything else and left.

When Mel heard the door at the top of the stairs close, she took a long look at the ring on her finger.

Finally, she cried.

Chapter Twenty

Night came.

Sterling felt every second of the lead-up. Every second that Mel was missing. Every second that someone else thought she was guilty.

Guilty of her ex-husband's crimes.

That angered Sterling to no end.

And was one of the reasons he was asked to leave the department and stay his ass at home.

"You are the only one here who hasn't even flinched at the onslaught of evidence coming in that, at the very least, might mean Melanie is working *with* a Partridge," Cole Reiner said when he was back from the hospital. He'd walked away from the crash with a broken arm and a well of anger. "Either now or back then. You're too close to this. You're too close to her. She could shoot you in the face at this point and I think you'd take it with the insistence that it wasn't her who'd done it."

Sterling's rage had been boiling at that.

Foster, who had run into a whole heap of red tape about trying to get visual confirmation that Rider Partridge was indeed in his cell and had headed to the prison several hours away himself, had been the only thing that had kept Sterling from making a true scene.

"No one can force you to stay at home, but you're going to have to leave your badge there," Foster had said when Sterling had called after his verbal tussle with Cole. "He's right, Sterling. You're only starting to make this harder for us and worse on yourself. That only hurts Melanie in the long run."

But no one knew where Mel was.

No one could tell him that she was okay.

That she wasn't hurt or scared or—

Sterling couldn't even think about the worst-case scenario.

He did, however, listen to his colleagues. Mainly because there was nothing else he could do at the department. He went home, changed into his boots and jeans, and dropped his badge at the door.

He kept his holster on, his gun inside.

Then he went to look for her himself.

Sterling drove to every place he could think of that either Partridge might go. That Mel might go. Then he thought about where she would look guiltiest if found.

That's why he went back to the Meeting House a second time just as the sun started to set.

Crime scene tape dressed the barely livable house. Sterling took out his flashlight and searched high and low throughout the structure. He even ducked to look beneath the foundation at the side of the porch.

It was why he didn't hear the man approach.

He did lift his gun in time to make the newcomer stop and raise his hands in defense.

Sterling recognized him instantly.

The man he'd shot at the Meeting House. The one no one had found.

"If you don't come with me, Melanie Blankenship will be killed," he said, no preamble. "You come now, no fuss, and that won't happen."

Sterling didn't lower his gun.

Though he did believe the man.

"Tell me this first—who are you working for?"

He wanted to be sure.

Not just have a theory.

The man, at the very least, obliged. He looked tired, worn. Seen much better days than the ones he was experiencing in Kelby Creek.

"We both know it's Rider," he answered. "And we both know he's back in town. So, let's not keep him waiting or that prized patience of his might just go to hell."

Sterling weighed his options, but it was like putting a feather on a scale against the weight of a building.

There was only one option for him.

"Lead the way."

STERLING GOT OUT of the Bronco and was staring at water.

And a dock that stretched over the darkness. Black glass surrounding the wood and quiet. There was a lone light on one of the wooden columns.

Mel was standing at the dock's end.

Alone.

Sterling gave his driver a long look.

The man nodded to Mel.

Only one of them had a gun now, and it certainly wasn't Sterling.

He wanted to tell the man something—anything—to get them out of the situation but knew there wasn't a word he could say against Rider to one of his lackeys.

So Sterling walked to the dock and focused on the relief filling his chest. If only for the moment.

Mel was alive and, as he got closer, seemed physically okay.

"Mel?"

He slowed his approach, boots thudding against the wood of the dock. Mel was standing awfully still.

She watched him with wide, tear-filled eyes.

"Rider's back." Her words were quiet. A drop in the creek around them.

Sterling stopped, a foot away from her. He nodded.

"I figured as much when the only other option was you were the bad guy."

Mel seemed surprised. She rattled on, voice shaking.

"I think Ella was in on it, too. Haven't seen Jonathan yet, but who knows where he is."

Sterling reached out. Mel took a small step back, her eyes widening again. This time in fear.

"Where's Rider? What's going on?" he asked. "Why are we here?"

Mel pointed down at a spot near their feet.

"He said this was the last stop on the tour."

The spot, like the rest of the dock, was dark from the wood being wet after the storm.

"We're near the house," he realized. The same house he should have known to check when Mel went missing. Sterling hadn't even made it an option in his mind since the house had already been used as a piece in Rider's game. He should have known the man would have doubled down on such an elaborate set piece. Because Rider was that dramatic. And Sterling should have realized that. Just as he finally understood something else. "This dock is close enough to kill someone and move them there by a quick car ride."

Mel nodded.

"This is where Rose was killed," Sterling continued. He sighed. "And this is where he wants you to kill me."

Mel let out a strangled sob.

She didn't correct him.

"I knew when they showed up for me. It's the only thing that makes sense." He gave her a small smile. "I've never not loved you, and I'd never not fight for you. Getting me out of the picture makes sense."

Tears started to fall down Mel's cheeks.

"Oh, Sterling. I'm so sorry," she cried. "It's all my fault. I never should have married him. I should have married you."

Sterling reached out again. This time Mel let him wrap his arms around her.

Mel's body shook against his.

"And I should have asked you to marry me," he said into her hair.

Her sobs became harder.

Sterling pulled away. He put his hands on the sides of her face to focus on her.

"None of this is your fault. Not one moment of it. Not back then, not now, not whatever happens next. Okay?"

The new position opened up room for him to see her hands pressed against her chest.

Sterling saw the ring first.

He dropped his hand to hers and pulled it out between them, cradling it as she shook.

"Where did you get this?"

Mel took a deep breath.

"Rider said I found it after the tornado. He—he kept it and put it on me at the house."

Her eyes searched his.

Sterling touched the ring.

The one he'd bought for her after their first kiss.

The one he'd never told her about.

"I should have been the one who put it on you." Sterling smiled. Mel's chest moved as she tried to control her crying. It wasn't the time, but he finally, truly understood what had happened back then. So much so he didn't even form it into a question. "You left town because Rider threatened me. He was using me against you. He's using me against you now." He let out a deep breath and looked around them. The man in the Bronco was still there. Waiting.

Sterling went back to the second thing he'd seen Mel holding.

He turned her hand over in his.

Beneath the engagement ring and against her palm was a full syringe.

"What does he want you to do now?" he asked.

Mel's tears were flowing now.

"I made a deal—deal with him." She shook her head. "I—I do this to you and—and—" A sob racked her body so hard that Sterling tightened his hold to steady her. It broke his heart when she met his eye again.

There was so much pain there.

And he was about to find out why he couldn't do a damn thing to stop it.

"It's okay," he told her. "It's okay."

Mel shook her head again. She took a moment to compose herself. It was still shaky, but when she spoke it was clear as day.

"He said there were only one or two people in this world that I'd burn everything for, and I thought there was only one. Only you. But, Sterling, he has Sam."

A gut punch unlike any other shook him.

Guilt as fierce as fire followed.

In all the madness, he hadn't once called Sam.

And Sam hadn't once called him.

He should have known.

"What's the deal you made?" Sterling kept his voice calm, low. The fear and rage wouldn't help Mel. It wouldn't help Sam. It wouldn't help Robbie or Linney.

Mel took a deep breath.

"Inject you and I can go back to the house and do the same to Sam. He won't remember what happened and—and I tell the cops everything that I did and admit I was the one who framed Rider after The Flood."

Sterling didn't think it was that easy.

Mel gave him an imploring look.

"He's been planning on me taking the fall for years. I believe him, Sterling. I believe him when he says he's thought of everything and can pin this on me. I believe him." Mel glanced down at the syringe. "I could have said no. But—but it's Sam."

Sterling let go of her hand and ran it across her cheek.

"And we can't let Sam die," he finished.

Sterling closed the space between them and gave Mel a long, deep kiss.

It felt like the first time.

Soft and warm and perfect.

When he broke it, Mel was crying again.

"I don't know what he has planned for you after," she said, shaking her head. "Maybe we can run? Jump in the water and swim away? Send the cavalry to the house? Maybe we—"

Sterling stepped back and took the syringe with him. He stuck it into his arm before she could stop him.

"Don't think for a second I'm going to let Rider Partridge keep us apart any longer. You save Sam, I'll save you. The details in between don't matter right now."

He pushed the plunger down. Small but necessary pain pinched beneath his skin.

Mel put her hands over her mouth.

Sterling pulled the syringe out and held it up in the air, turning to motion to their friend at the Bronco.

He was on the phone.

He nodded.

Sterling turned back to Mel.

She was so scared.

Sterling smiled.

He took her hand again.

"Can you do me a favor?"

Mel's lip quivered. She nodded.

"Anything."

Sterling thumbed the engagement ring.

"I want to ask you to marry me, but I'm afraid I'll forget I did it when this has gone through my system. So." He tapped the ring. "The next time you see me, make Sam give this to me and I promise I'll give it right back. Deal?"

An unfamiliar sensation started to run down his back.

One not so unfamiliar wrapped around his heart when Mel reached for him. Her kiss was quick and hard.

The sound of approaching footfalls didn't help.

She looked over his shoulder.

Then back to him one last time.

She smiled. It was small, tired, afraid, but genuine.

"I'll say yes."

Sterling let her go as the man from the Bronco took the syringe with gloved hands.

"Time to go," he told Mel.

And she did.

And Sterling was glad for it.

He watched as they got into the Bronco and drove away.

Then he tried to hurry, to escape whatever was supposed to happen next, but all he did was go numb at the first step off the dock.

Sterling went to his knees as a man appeared out of the darkness near him.

Sterling balled his fists.

He might be down, but he certainly wasn't out.

Not yet.

Chapter Twenty-One

Mel couldn't see through her tears as the night swam past the Bronco's windows.

She'd killed Sterling.

She'd killed the man she loved because of the man she never should have married.

It was all her fault, no matter what he'd said.

The sob that tore from her mouth shook the man next to her.

He actually jumped.

"Man, I felt that all the way in my toes."

Mel folded in on herself. Her head went to her knees, her arms wrapped around her stomach.

The man didn't speak for a second. His tone changed when he did.

"You coulda run with him, you know," he said. "I mean, I would have tried to stop you two, but I've seen how fast that man is and there's a good chance y'all coulda escaped. Why didn't you? Why didn't you even try?"

Mel shook her head.

Then she was back to sitting up, wiping her eyes with the back of her arm, astonished at the question.

"Because Rider has Sam," she said simply.

The man's eyebrow rose.

When Sam had been brought into the basement, the man in the fisherman's cap had done it. Mel had yelled at him, angry and afraid for Sam. He'd been bloodied and stumbling. Like a true Costner, he'd tried to assure *her* that *he* was okay while being forced into cuffs on the chair she'd just been freed from.

He'd also been insistent that she not do anything Rider said.

When she'd agreed to inject Sterling with the Sleepers drug so the final piece of evidence could be thrown against her, Sam had all but screamed.

But he wouldn't remember that she'd made the call. Not once the Sleepers went into his system.

He'd just wake up one day, confused and lost without his big brother.

"Oh God," Mel let out. "Sam will never forgive me."

The man behind the wheel wasn't connecting any dots.

"Who the hell is Sam? Is that another lover of yours?"

Had it been any other situation, Mel wouldn't have dignified him with a response to a question so personal.

Now, now part of her world was about to end, so she told the truth.

"Sam is Sterling's little brother." Anger, rage flew hot and fast through her, burning out the urge to keep crying. "Rider said he picked me to marry because I only truly loved two people in this world. Two people he could use against me if he ever needed to do something like this." Mel hit the dash. "He gave me a choice—Sterling for Sam, and once I told Sterling that…it wasn't a choice anymore. They're my two people, and Sam and I are Sterling's. We lose saving Sam. Sterling loses more by not saving him. I knew that. I *know* that."

Her hand hurt at the hit. Mel flexed it. She got caught looking at the ring.

Her emotions were tangling together as they drove back to the house.

"Rider has spent his adulthood trying to be the best of the best—trying to be king." Mel shook her head. "He knew that Sterling would make the choice for me, but he'll never *truly* understand why he made it."

She turned to the man.

The gun at his hip wasn't the one he'd used to shoot Ella—the one with her fingerprints on it. Mel didn't know where that gun had gone, but she was sure it was somewhere waiting to implicate her.

"Rider doesn't see us. He only sees how he can use us. He doesn't care what happens when that use is done."

The man met her gaze. Mel was so close to him that his dark eyes reflected a startling movement.

They were driving up to the house.

Rider's castle.

Mel whirled around.

Flames.

They were crawling up the front of the house.

"No! Sam!"

The man stopped the car, but Mel was already out and running.

She tore through the front yard like a bat out of hell. The flames weren't high, but they were eating away at the front porch and exterior of the first floor and main door. So she ran full tilt to the back.

The gate to the yard was locked.

Mel scrambled to jump the wrought iron.

Pain scored her as the iron cut open her shin.

She didn't care.

She didn't need to know Rider's plan to know that Sam was still in that basement.

Still tied up.

Mel landed on the grass and picked up speed to the back door that led into the kitchen.

It was locked, but it gave very little resistance to the rusty fire poker that had lain useless for five years near the fire pit off the porch. The glass shattered with ease. Mel ran it around the rim until most of the glass was gone. She felt more pain as she scrambled through it. A piece had cut her. Just as the fence had.

She didn't care.

"Sam?" she yelled into the kitchen.

Mel regretted it.

Smoke was already spreading through the bottom floor of the house. Her eyes watered while she coughed into her arm.

The door to the basement was the only hurdle she didn't have to jump. It was wide-open.

Mel saved her breath and hurried down the stairs.

Briefly she thought that Sam wasn't there. That Rider had kept true to his word and burning down the house was just another step in the plan to have all clues pointing to her guilt.

Then she saw him at the back of the room.

His head was hanging low.

He wasn't moving.

"Sam!"

Mel rushed over, true terror in her heart.

She could have flown when she saw his chest rise with breath.

Mel tried to wake him, but he was limp. A small blood mark was on his right arm.

Rider had drugged him.

And he was still handcuffed to the chair.

Mel dug her hands into the cuffs, trying to free him. When they didn't budge, she tried it in reverse. They were so tight against his skin there was no wiggle room. She turned her attention to the chair. She pulled on the wooden arm that the cuff was clasped around. It, too, didn't budge.

So Mel pushed the chair over.

"Sorry," she told the unconscious Sam. His body jostled to the floor while the hand attached by the cuff swung above him.

Mel had never been a tall woman but with the chair on its side, she had just enough space to kick her foot forward. The first time she missed, but the second time her heel connected with the chair arm.

To her absolute delight, she felt it give.

The wood might have been expensive, but the frame beneath the fabric only took four solid kicks to break. Several moments later Mel took that broken piece and snapped it the rest of the way off, with the cuff attached to Sam.

His arm dropped like a ton of bricks.

Him helping her help *him* was out of the question.

Mel moved her hair back, sweat and blood soaking her clothes. She was tired. She hurt. But she wasn't about to give up.

Bending low, she grabbed Sam's hands and started to pull.

He didn't move much.

"Come on," she yelled at herself.

Mel adjusted her hold and pulled with all her might. Sam, thankfully, followed this time. It was excruciatingly slow. At this rate she'd make it to the stairs just as the fire did. Never mind going up them.

Somewhere above them, the house made an awful noise.

Mel kept pulling.

She couldn't let Sam die. Not after Sterling had—

"Move."

The voice was deep and commanding. The push at her side was gentle.

Mel was shocked to see the man from the Bronco.

He looked the worst he had since she'd been taken by him that morning.

"Come on."

He scooped Sam up and threw him over his shoulder like a sack of flour. Mel didn't ask questions. She followed him up the stairs and went around him to open the back door in the kitchen.

The smoke was thick now, dark and hot.

They ran into the backyard, coughing.

After a few yards, the man lowered Sam to the ground. Mel was on him in an instant.

Still breathing.

Mel turned her attention to the man. She didn't know why he'd helped her, but she was grateful.

"Thank you," she said, meaning every word. "Thank you so much."

The man shrugged off his deed.

"I'm not a good man, but I can still see people as human beings."

Mel felt absolute fondness for the man.

It was partly why she yelled when the gunshot tore through him. He crumpled to the ground before she could spot who'd done it. Mel threw herself over Sam just in case more shots came.

The shooter merely laughed.

"You know, this is actually perfect."

Rider lowered his gun.

"Did you know that Westley here is who I planned to make your accomplice? Because, as much as you've done in town, you'd need at least one person to help you. It was going to be Dewey, but he went and got himself in the hospital. So Westley here got an upgrade to a big-time role…and he didn't even know it. I was going to kill him before that. But now, look at this absolute gift."

The sound of fire crackling behind him, the sight of smoke billowing high, gave Rider the look of a devil in his delight.

"The theatrics of the last week have almost made the last five years in prison worth it."

"The theatrics?"

Mel thought of Rose Simon, dead in their old bed. The shoot-out at the Meeting House. Abducted after a tornado. She thought of the sheriff and his heart attack. Detective Reiner unmoving in the front seat of a crashed car. The man named Westley whose change of heart had saved a drugged Sam.

She thought of Sterling and the ring on her finger.

This was a play to Rider. A game. A chessboard where no one moved their piece without him punishing them for it.

Mel thought of Annie McHale, trapped in the basement just below their feet. Terrified and alone.

Then she looked up at the man who didn't seem real. A nightmare come to life.

It was then that she finally saw it.

The lie.

Mel stood, slowly.

Rider found humor in it. The ant that dared bare its chest at the boot.

He was about to regret that smug look.

"You're called the Connected Corruptor because you made sure everyone stayed in charge." Mel stepped over Sam. She stood a few feet from Rider. "Everyone *else*. You were the tape, the glue. You were a tool. I'm not sure if anyone has ever told you this, but you were never in charge of anything, and I don't know why it's taken me so long to realize it. Just like I don't think the flaw in your precious plan of making me the bad guy has ever crossed your mind."

Rider's smug smile turned into an angry frown.

She'd struck a nerve.

"What flaw?" he asked.

Mel smiled.

"Make me the villain and I just might play the part."

Mel lunged forward and used her right palm to thrust Rider's hand up. The gun he was holding went off but flew out of his grip after. Mel's attention had already split. Her left hand went flat against his chest with all the force she could muster. Rider, a man who'd never fought—something he paid others to do—lost his footing. He didn't fall, but the stumble was enough of an opening. Mel brought her right hand back again, but this time she balled it and punched him in the face.

She missed but had already committed to ending this. Following her momentum, she spun around and used her left elbow as her next attack.

It landed against his chin.

Rider made a pathetic cry of pain.

That only enthused Mel. She pulled back to continue her onslaught but was caught off guard by movement over his shoulder.

It made her hesitate.

Which was enough time for Rider to show Mel one last time that he never played fair.

The gun she'd knocked out of his hand wasn't the only one he'd had.

Rider pulled it up and aimed. Mel fell back against the grass trying to dodge the shot.

Mel closed her eyes tight.

The gunshot tore through the night air, the sound of flames as its backdrop.

Mel waited for the pain. Waited for the darkness.

Yet it never came.

She opened her eyes just in time to watch Rider fall forward.

Behind him was the movement she'd seen before.

A man with a gun.

"Sterling!"

Sterling dropped to his knees, the gun dropping from his hand.

Mel flew up, kicked Rider's gun clear across the grass and was on Sterling in a flash.

"Sterling!" She wrapped her arms around the man and felt his whole weight press into her. It made them both fall flat.

Mel scrambled to sit back up. She held his back against her chest.

"Are you—are you okay?" he asked. His words were soft. Low.

Mel nodded. She looked down and saw blood on him. She couldn't tell where it was coming from. Instead she answered him, relief that he was here flowing through her.

"Now I am."

"Sam?"

"He's good, too. Just sleeping."

Sterling's head was starting to droop.

The drugs were finally pulling him under.

She barely heard his last words.

"I think I might, too."

Chapter Twenty-Two

Sterling woke up warm.

With his eyes closed, he thought of Mel next to him in bed. He almost let sleep take him back under, but then there was the beeping. Then a dull pain in the back of his head.

He opened his eyes and found himself in a hospital bed, two thick blankets on top of him. Not Mel.

She was on the couch next to his bed.

There was a baby in her arms.

Sterling moved, and Mel's gaze was quick.

She smiled.

Sterling had no idea what had landed him in the hospital, but that smile put him right at ease.

"I'm guessin' something happened," he said after a moment.

Mel's smile grew, but her words were quiet.

"You definitely could say that." She didn't try to stand but did angle her body so she could face him easier. Sterling could see the baby's face now. It was Linney. "Don't worry," Mel hurriedly tacked on. "Everyone is fine now. I'm just giving Sam and Robbie a little time alone. I figured you wouldn't mind."

Sterling had questions, but it seemed like the right thing to do was not ask them now. Instead he watched Mel readjust the sleeping Linney.

He liked the sight.

"How are you feeling?" Mel asked when Linney didn't wake.

Sterling thought about it a moment.

"Laggy," he decided. "Fuzzy. Like I woke up from sleep too fast and I could go back in a second."

He yawned, proving his point.

A look of concern crossed her brow, but Mel didn't sound it.

"The doctor said your dosage was a lot higher than ours. He said you might wake and sleep a few times before finally being able to stay up. Do you want to sleep some more?"

He did, but worry caught him.

"Will you be here when I wake up?"

Mel didn't skip a beat.

"I haven't left you yet."

Sterling didn't say she had before. He closed his eyes and let sleep drag him under again.

THE NEXT TIME he woke, Mel was still on the couch. This time she was asleep. A nurse talked softly to him, and a doctor came in after that. He got up after that, slow but steady, and used the bathroom. He showered and found a change of clothes folded in the corner. He did all movements with caution and was just as slow when he went back out to the room.

Mel was waiting for him. She had a pillow mark lining her cheek. Sterling smiled at it. At her.

"You stayed."

Mel laughed.

"And you got right up to walking around. You must be feeling better."

She stepped back to the couch, and Sterling lowered himself into the seat next to her. He flinched at the pain in his ribs. Mel didn't miss it.

"I guess that means you might be up to hearing what happened."

"I wouldn't mind a play-by-play."

Mel tilted her head, blue eyes clear.

"What *is* the last thing you remember? For everyone else it's been different."

Sterling had thought about that in the shower. Now that he was feeling more like himself, the answer was the same as it had been earlier.

"You," he said. "Next to me in bed."

Mel's cheeks went rosy. She dipped her chin a little.

"Not a bad memory to take a pause at, if you ask me," he added.

Sterling took her chin in his hand and pulled her to his lips.

She let the movement happen.

The kiss was quiet. Calm.

When it ended, it ended too soon.

"I've been told I'm missing close to two days of memory, but I sure hope I did that sometime in between."

Mel sighed. A smile was still there when the breath was gone.

"A lot happened—not all of it good, but some of it definitely so."

She took his hand in hers.

"But not all of it is mine to tell. We need to bring in some more people to get the whole picture."

THE WHOLE PICTURE went from the two of them in his hospital room to two more. Detective Reiner had a cast on. Sam had a hospital band on his wrist. Mel started as soon as they were seated.

The story started with Cole showing up at the house. It nose-dived after that.

"Deputy Park found me unconscious and James shot on the ground next to the car," Reiner said when she got to his part. "He was wearing a vest but pretty banged up. He told us that Jonathan Partridge had rammed into us and had worked with Mel to escape. Then shot him when he tried to fight back."

"When really it was the man from the Meeting House, Westley, who grabbed me and shot James, who, by the way, volunteered for the bullet," Mel added.

"After that the department got word that the Bronco with Jonathan and Mel had gone downtown and shot Ella Cochlin," Reiner continued. "Around the same time you blew through the department to Foster and pitched your theory that Mel was being set up by Rider, and if Rider was setting her up, then he had to be in town."

Sterling nodded to his own deduction. It made sense,

especially since there was no way that Mel had done any of what she'd been accused of doing.

"Foster believed you and drove out to the prison to see for himself."

"Oh, and the man from the Meeting House woke up here in the hospital, saying that Rider was innocent," Mel interjected. "I wasn't personally here for that, but Detective Lovett gave me the full rundown earlier."

Cole nodded.

"By the time Foster made it to the prison and saw that Rider had switched places with a man named Randy Kolt and paid off several guards *heavily*, we realized that you'd gone missing, too."

"Before that Westley had already taken me to a house out near the creek for a bad guy monologue," Mel jumped in. "Then he took me to the house and a basement full of his supply of Sleepers."

Sam raised his hand.

"That's where I come in, apparently. Robbie said they found my car still running outside Sterling's place, empty. That other guy got me, as far as they can tell."

Sterling became angry again. Mel touched his hand.

"The other guy was another Rider lackey. His name was Bailey, and he owned the fisherman's cabin I woke up in after being taken the first time," she explained. "He didn't mind at all doing the things Rider paid him to do."

"His name *was*? Is he dead?"

Cole and Mel shared a look. Sam nodded.

"They'll get to that. This is the part you're going to

want to hear first." Sam nodded to Mel. This time they shared the look. It was soft but warm.

Then she told him about their time at the dock. The deal she'd made and how Sterling had been the one to finish it by injecting himself.

Mel's eyes had started to water. This time he took her hand and squeezed.

"I don't remember it happening, but I stand by what we both did," he told her. "What happened after you and Westley left?"

Mel shook her head a little and cleared her throat.

"Bailey showed up to try and kill you," Cole said. He laughed. "You're never going to believe who helped save you."

Sterling had no idea. He said as much.

Sam couldn't keep it in.

"It was Jonathan Partridge," he said, a little too loud.

Sterling didn't believe him.

"No way."

"Yep," Mel responded. "Jonathan Partridge showed up, helped you fight off Bailey and then drove you to the house while calling in the entire department."

"Hearing you back up the story on speakerphone definitely helped," Cole added.

After that the story became no less wild. Jonathan had apparently gone into the house to make sure no one was in the basement while Sterling had fought the drugs in his system long enough to run outside when he heard Rider shoot Westley.

"The doctors said it was a miracle you hung on as

long as you did," Mel said quietly. "Rider didn't plan on that."

But he had. Long enough to save Mel.

That made simple sense to him, too.

The story wrapped up in technical details. Jonathan had run out to greet the arriving deputies and firemen, and Sterling, Sam and Westley had been transported to the hospital. Rider hadn't survived the shot. They all took a moment of silence for that but didn't linger on it.

While everyone was in the hospital, the house burned to the ground. Later a rumor would start that the structure could have been saved but instead the fire department and deputies alike watched it burn, standing on the front lawn, ash falling around them. He'd never know if it was true or not, because no one talked about the house ever again.

Ella Cochlin and Deputy James Reynolds recovered quickly from their respective wounds while Sterling and Sam slept off their drugs. The moment they found out Rider had passed, they both broke down. Ella had been in a relationship with Rider after a chance encounter with him while visiting her brother in prison. Since then she had made her home in Kelby Creek and waited to be another thing that tried to make Mel look guilty. James, however, had been blackmailed for almost as long. He'd been one of the few who had been protected by Rider's omission of facts during the investigation after The Flood. The same went for the man who had owned the fishing cabin, Bailey. He'd died of his wounds inflicted in the fight with Sterling and Jonathan, but Ella had told his story in full.

Then there was the man who had fallen into a coma after the Meeting House. He was the son of Randy Kolt, the man who'd switched places with Rider at the prison. He never would admit why he'd helped Rider, but there was enough on him that he was about to go to prison himself.

The only person left who had helped spin the web surrounding Mel was a man Sterling visited before he was discharged later that week.

Westley looked awful.

It was a miracle he was even alive, though that miracle was mostly due to the fact that Rider Partridge was a terrible shot.

"Three bullets I've taken in this town. I'm going to laugh if anyone tries to tell me Kelby Creek ain't dangerous again."

Sterling had laughed at that and sat with the man awhile. He had already agreed to cooperate fully in the investigation and had evidence that damned everyone involved. Including himself.

All Sterling could do, though, was thank him for saving his brother.

"Don't thank me," he'd said, serious. "You thank that woman of yours. She's the one who ran into a burning building to save someone you loved."

Sterling had left him at that, promising that he and Mel would make it known how Westley had helped, and Mel and Sterling finally went home.

Before he could get down to something else he'd been wanting to talk to her about, someone else came calling for a chat.

Jonathan Partridge had definitely seen better days. Scabbed and bruised and limping, he took a seat at the kitchen table and finally gave Sterling the rest of the missing pieces.

"Everyone assumed I was always with Rider just because I was his brother. Even you, which I think is why I was so angry with you all these years." He said the last part to Mel and gave her a sympathetic smile. "You knew me, and the second Rider was found guilty, you joined everyone else in pointing the finger at me because I was blood. I should have told you in no uncertain terms that I wasn't but, well, pride, I guess."

Mel apologized to him then and there. Sterling, too. Jonathan shrugged it off but accepted.

"I tried to believe he was good, but after the trial and all the evidence, well, I cut him off," he continued. "Every month for five years he called me and punished me for it. Asked if the town still hated me for something I never did. Every month without fail. Made me furious because I never could escape that call. He always found a way. Then, one month, the call didn't come. At least not from him."

"Rose," Mel offered. Jonathan nodded.

"She told me that she was being forced to write a new piece on Rider on the anniversary of The Flood. That it was an entire spread about how Mel was the real Connected Corruptor and that Rose had been wrong. But whatever he had on Rose wasn't enough to bind her conscience. She reached out to me because she's the only one who always believed I had nothing to do with it. Then I reached out to you."

Mel had already heard the story from Jonathan in the hospital, but Sterling put it all together for the first time now.

"You're why Mel came back to town."

Again, Jonathan nodded.

"We decided to meet with Rose at the Meeting House, but on the way into town Rose had a change of heart," he said. "So Mel and I decided to head to the sheriff's department instead. For whatever reason, Rose turned on us. We fought, and Bailey showed up. He managed to drug Mel before we got away, but they chased us down."

"That's when the car accident happened," Sterling realized. "And it was you driving."

"Yep. And what a job I did."

Mel had swatted at him, affection clear in her voice.

"He convinced Bailey that if they took me then and there that his brother's plan of framing me wouldn't work. Instead putting me as the driver would work the best. Then he went to check on me at the hospital."

Jonathan shrugged.

"I didn't know what they'd given her, but when I realized her memory was gone, I panicked and worried that she wouldn't believe me without Rose. So I left to try and get some proof. I couldn't find it, but once I heard that you had gone missing, I went to where I thought Rose might have been killed. That's when I found you."

Mel had surprised them both by hugging Jonathan tight at that. Sterling surprised himself by not being far behind.

Jonathan had laughed when they saw him out to the front porch.

"I know this might come off as a weird thing to say, but I've always thought you two made a much better couple."

He told them 'bye and drove off, lighter than when he'd walked in.

Then it was Sterling and Mel.

She sighed her way into the comfort of the couch. Sterling followed suit.

"You know, while I was talking to Sheriff Chamblin and his wife at the hospital, they invited us over to their house for some good ol' comfort food since he's now officially on the mend," Mel said. "And Lordy if that doesn't sound good after the last two weeks."

She had her eyes closed and was feeling a sigh.

Sterling angled his body to face her and held up something for her to see.

When she opened those blue eyes he'd loved since he was a teen, they went right to the ring in his hand.

"Sam said you gave this to him when he woke up," he started. "He said you swore him to secrecy on how it ended up on your finger. I'm not going to ask about that now, because, well, I'm going to kiss the person right in front of me." Sterling smiled.

"I'd like to ask you to marry me, though, right here and now. Maybe even for a second time, because, well, it's hard not to love you out loud, and I'm tired of pretending I'm okay with not being with you." He held the ring out, heartbeat already in sync with hers. "What do you think?"

Mel looked at the ring. Then her eyelashes fluttered up and those blue eyes were his.

"You can ask me every day for the rest of our lives and I'll always say yes to loving you, Sterling Costner."

She let him put the ring on her finger.

Then she kissed him long and true.

Later that month they'd marry on the back porch of the house, Sam between them as he officiated the wedding. They'd never remember the memories they'd lost but they didn't need them to know they were lucky, all things considered. After the ceremony Sterling and Mel would drive off to their honeymoon, but not before stopping for slushies.

Then it was just like they were teens again, driving around with the breeze in their hair and love in their hearts.

* * * * *

Don't miss the next book in
Tyler Anne Snell's Saving Kelby Creek series
when Cold Case Captive *goes on sale in June 2022.*

And look for the previous books in the series:

Uncovering Small Town Secrets
Searching for Evidence
Surviving the Truth

Available now wherever
Harlequin Intrigue books are sold!

WE HOPE YOU ENJOYED THIS BOOK FROM

⊕HARLEQUIN

INTRIGUE

Seek thrills. Solve crimes. Justice served.

Dive into action-packed stories that will keep you
on the edge of your seat. Solve the crime
and deliver justice at all costs.

6 NEW BOOKS AVAILABLE EVERY MONTH!

HIHALO2020

COMING NEXT MONTH FROM

⧫ HARLEQUIN

INTRIGUE

#2073 STICKING TO HER GUNS
A Colt Brothers Investigation • by B.J. Daniels

Tommy Colt is stunned when his childhood best friend—and love—
Bella Worthington abruptly announces she's engaged to their old-time nemesis!
Knowing her better than anyone, Tommy's convinced something is dangerously
wrong. Now Colt Brothers Investigations' newest partner is racing to uncover the
truth and ask Bella a certain question...if they survive.

#2074 FOOTHILLS FIELD SEARCH
K-9s on Patrol • by Maggie Wells

When two kids are kidnapped from plain sight, Officer Brady Nichols and his
intrepid canine, Winnie, spring into action. Single mother Cassie Whitaker thought
she'd left big-city peril behind—until it followed her to Jasper. But can Brady and
his K-9 protect Cassie from a stalker who won't take no for an answer?

#2075 NEWLYWED ASSIGNMENT
A Ree and Quint Novel • by Barb Han

Hardheaded ATF legend Quint Casey knows he's playing with fire asking
Agent Ree Sheppard to re-up as his undercover wife. To crack a ruthless Houston
weapons ring, they must keep the mission—and their explosive chemistry—under
control. But Quint's determined need for revenge and Ree's risky moves are
putting everything on the line...

#2076 UNDERCOVER RESCUE
A North Star Novel Series • by Nicole Helm

After the husband she thought was dead returns with revenge on his mind,
Veronica Shay resolves to confront her secret past—and her old boss,
Granger Macmillan, won't let her handle it on her own. But when they fall into a
nefarious trap, they'll call in their entire North Star family in order to stay alive...

#2077 COLD CASE CAPTIVE
The Saving Kelby Creek Series • by Tyler Anne Snell

Returning to Kelby Creek only intensifies Detective Lily Howard's guilt at the
choice she made years ago to rescue her childhood crush, Anthony Perez, rather
than pursue the man abducting his sister. But another teen girl's disappearance
offers a chance to work with Ant again—and a tantalizing new lead that could
mean inescapable danger.

#2078 THE HEART-SHAPED MURDERS
A West Coast Crime Story • by Denise N. Wheatley

Attacked and left with a partial heart-shaped symbol carved into her chest,
forensic investigator Lena Love finds leaving LA to return to her hometown comes
with its own danger—like detective David Hudson, the love she left behind.
But soon bodies—all marked with the killer's signature heart—are discovered in
David's jurisdiction...

**YOU CAN FIND MORE INFORMATION ON UPCOMING HARLEQUIN TITLES,
FREE EXCERPTS AND MORE AT HARLEQUIN.COM.**

HICNM0422

*Wedding bells and shotgun fire are ringing out
in Lonesome, Montana. Read on for another
Colt Brothers Investigation novel from* New York Times
bestselling author B.J. Daniels.

Bella Worthington took a breath and, opening her eyes, finally faced her
reflection in the full-length mirror. The wedding dress fit perfectly—just as
he'd said it would. While accentuating her curves, the neckline was modest,
the drape flattering. As much as she hated to admit it, Fitz had good taste.

The sapphire-and-diamond necklace he'd given her last night gleamed
at her throat, bringing out the blue-green of her eyes—also like he'd said
it would. He'd thought of everything—right down to the huge pear-shaped
diamond engagement ring on her finger. All of it would be sold off before the
ink dried on the marriage license—if she let it go that far.

As she studied her reflection, though, she realized this was exactly as
he'd planned it. She looked the beautiful bride on her wedding day. No one
would be the wiser.

She could hear music and the murmur of voices downstairs. He'd invited
the whole town of Lonesome, Montana. She'd watched from the upstairs
window as the guests had arrived earlier. He'd wanted an audience for this
and now he would have one.

The knock at the door startled her, even though she'd been expecting
it. "It's time," said a male voice on the other side. One of Fitz's hired
bodyguards, Ronan, was waiting. He would be carrying a weapon under his
suit. Security, she'd been told, to keep her safe. A lie.

She listened as Ronan unlocked her door and waited outside, his boss
not taking any chances. He had made sure there was no possibility of escape
short of shackling her to her bed. Fitz was determined that she find no way
out of this. It didn't appear that she had.

In a few moments, she would be escorted downstairs to where her maid
of honor and bridesmaids were waiting—all handpicked by her groom. If
they'd questioned why they were down there and she was up here, they
hadn't asked. He wasn't the kind of man women questioned. At least not
more than once.

For another moment, Bella stared at the stranger in the mirror. She didn't
have to wonder how she'd gotten to this point in her life. Unfortunately, she

knew too well. She'd just never thought Fitz would go this far. Her mistake. He, however, had no idea how far she was willing to go to make sure the wedding never happened.

Taking a breath, she picked up her bouquet from her favorite local flower shop. The bouquet had been a special order delivered earlier. Her hand barely trembled as she lifted the blossoms to her nose for a moment, taking in the sweet scent of the tiny white roses—also his choice. Carefully, she separated the tiny buds, afraid it wouldn't be there.

It took her a few moments to find the long, slim silver blade hidden among the roses and stems. The blade was sharp, and lethal if used correctly. She knew exactly how to use it. She slid it back into the bouquet out of sight. He wouldn't think to check it. She hoped. He'd anticipated her every move and attacked with one of his own. Did she really think he wouldn't be ready for anything?

Making sure the door was still closed, she checked her garter. What she'd tucked under it was still there, safe, at least for the moment.

Another knock at the door. Fitz would be getting impatient and no one wanted that. "Everyone's waiting," Ronan said, tension in his tone. If this didn't go as meticulously planned, there would be hell to pay from his boss. Something else they all knew.

She stepped to the door and opened it, lifting her chin and straightening her spine. Ronan's eyes swept over her with a lusty gaze, but he stepped back as if not all that sure of her. Clearly he'd been warned to be wary of her. Probably just as she'd been warned what would happen if she refused to come down—or worse, made a scene in front of the guests.

At the bottom of the stairs, the room opened and she saw Fitz waiting for her with the person he'd hired to officiate.

He was so confident that he'd backed her into a corner with no way out. He'd always underestimated her. Today would be no different. But he didn't know her as well as he thought. He'd held her prisoner, threatened her, forced her into this dress and this ruse.

But that didn't mean she was going to marry him.

She would kill him first.

Don't miss
Sticking to Her Guns *by B.J. Daniels,*
available June 2022 wherever
Harlequin books and ebooks are sold.

Harlequin.com

Copyright © 2022 by Barbara Heinlein

HIEXP0322INC

Get 4 FREE REWARDS!

We'll send you 2 FREE Books plus 2 FREE Mystery Gifts.

KENTUCKY CRIME RING
JULIE ANNE LINDSEY

TEXAS STALKER
BARB HAN

FREE
Value Over
$20

UNDER THE RANCHER'S PROTECTION
ADDISON FOX

OPERATION WHISTLEBLOWER
JUSTINE DAVIS

Both the **Harlequin Intrigue**® and **Harlequin**® Romantic Suspense series feature compelling novels filled with heart-racing action-packed romance that will keep you on the edge of your seat.

YES! Please send me 2 FREE novels from the Harlequin Intrigue or Harlequin Romantic Suspense series and my 2 FREE gifts (gifts are worth about $10 retail). After receiving them, if I don't wish to receive any more books, I can return the shipping statement marked "cancel." If I don't cancel, I will receive 6 brand-new Harlequin Intrigue Larger-Print books every month and be billed just $5.99 each in the U.S. or $6.49 each in Canada, a savings of at least 14% off the cover price or 4 brand-new Harlequin Romantic Suspense books every month and be billed just $4.99 each in the U.S. or $5.74 each in Canada, a savings of at least 13% off the cover price. It's quite a bargain! Shipping and handling is just 50¢ per book in the U.S. and $1.25 per book in Canada.* I understand that accepting the 2 free books and gifts places me under no obligation to buy anything. I can always return a shipment and cancel at any time. The free books and gifts are mine to keep no matter what I decide.

Choose one: ☐ **Harlequin Intrigue**
Larger-Print
(199/399 HDN GNXC)

☐ **Harlequin Romantic Suspense**
(240/340 HDN GNMZ)

Name (please print)

Address   Apt. #

City   State/Province   Zip/Postal Code

Email: Please check this box ☐ if you would like to receive newsletters and promotional emails from Harlequin Enterprises ULC and its affiliates. You can unsubscribe anytime.

Mail to the **Harlequin Reader Service:**
IN U.S.A.: P.O. Box 1341, Buffalo, NY 14240-8531
IN CANADA: P.O. Box 603, Fort Erie, Ontario L2A 5X3

Want to try 2 free books from another series? Call 1-800-873-8635 or visit www.ReaderService.com.

*Terms and prices subject to change without notice. Prices do not include sales taxes, which will be charged (if applicable) based on your state or country of residence. Canadian residents will be charged applicable taxes. Offer not valid in Quebec. This offer is limited to one order per household. Books received may not be as shown. Not valid for current subscribers to the Harlequin Intrigue or Harlequin Romantic Suspense series. All orders subject to approval. Credit or debit balances in a customer's account(s) may be offset by any other outstanding balance owed by or to the customer. Please allow 4 to 6 weeks for delivery. Offer available while quantities last.

Your Privacy—Your information is being collected by Harlequin Enterprises ULC, operating as Harlequin Reader Service. For a complete summary of the information we collect, how we use this information and to whom it is disclosed, please visit our privacy notice located at corporate.harlequin.com/privacy-notice. From time to time we may also exchange your personal information with reputable third parties. If you wish to opt out of this sharing of your personal information, please visit readerservice.com/consumerschoice or call 1-800-873-8635. **Notice to California Residents**—Under California law, you have specific rights to control and access your data. For more information on these rights and how to exercise them, visit corporate.harlequin.com/california-privacy.

HIHRS22

SPECIAL EXCERPT FROM

H HARLEQUIN

INTRIGUE

*After forensic investigator Lena Love is attacked and
left with a partial heart-shaped symbol carved into her
chest, her hunt to find a serial killer becomes personal.*

Read on for a sneak preview of
The Heart-Shaped Murders,
*the debut book in A West Coast Crime Story series,
from Denise N. Wheatley.*

Lena Love kicked a rock out from underneath her foot, then
bent down and tightened the twill shoelaces on her brown
leather hiking boots.

The crime scene investigator, who doubled as a forensic
science technician, stood back up and eyed Los Angeles's
Cucamonga Wilderness trail. Sharp-edged stones and ragged
shards of bark covered the rugged, winding terrain.

"Watch your step," she uttered to herself before continuing
along the path of her latest crime scene.

Lena squinted as she focused on the trail. Heavy foliage
loomed overhead, blocking out the sun's brilliant rays. She
pulled out her flashlight, hoping its bright beam would help
uncover potential evidence.

An ominous wave of vulnerability swept through her
chest at the sight of the vast San Gabriel Mountains. She spun
around slowly, feeling small while eyeing the infinite views
of the forest, desert and snowy mountainous peaks.

The wild surroundings left her with a lingering sense of
defenselessness. Lena tightened the belt on her tan suede
blazer. She hoped it would give her some semblance of
security.

It didn't.

Lena wondered if the latest victim had felt that same vulnerability on the night she'd been brutally murdered.

"Come on, Grace Mitchell," Lena said aloud, as if the dead woman could hear her. "Talk to me. Tell me what happened to you. *Show* me what happened to you."

A gust of wind whipped Lena's bone-straight bob across her slender face. She tucked her hair behind her ears and stooped down, aiming the flashlight toward the majestic oak tree where Grace's body had been found.

Lena envisioned spotting droplets of blood, a cigarette butt, the tip of a latex glove…*anything* that would help identify the killer.

This was her second visit to the crime scene. The thought of showing up to the station without any viable evidence yet again caused an agonizing pang of dread to shoot up her spine.

Grace was the fifth victim of a criminal whom Lena had labeled an organized serial killer. He appeared to have a type. Young, slender brunette women. Their bodies had all been found in heavily wooded areas. Each victim's hands were meticulously tied behind their backs with a three-strand twisted rope. They'd been strangled to death. And the amount of evidence left at each scene was practically nonexistent.

But the killer's signature mark was always there. And it was a sinister one.

Look for
The Heart-Shaped Murders *by Denise N. Wheatley,*
available June 2022 wherever
Harlequin Intrigue books and ebooks are sold.

Harlequin.com

Copyright © 2022 by Denise N. Wheatley